美國英語閱讀課本 4
各學科實用課文 二版

+ Workbook

AMERICAN SCHOOL TEXTBOOK
READING KEY

作者 Michael A. Putlack & e-Creative Contents 譯者 丁宥暄

如何下載 **MP3** 音檔

❶ 寂天雲 APP 聆聽：掃描書上 QR Code 下載「寂天雲 - 英日語學習隨身聽」APP。加入會員後，用 APP 內建掃描器再次掃描書上 QR Code，即可使用 APP 聆聽音檔。

❷ 官網下載音檔：請上「寂天閱讀網」（www.icosmos.com.tw），註冊會員／登入後，搜尋本書，進入本書頁面，點選「MP3 下載」下載音檔，存於電腦等其他播放器聆聽使用。

The Best Preparation for Building Academic Reading Skills and Vocabulary

The Reading Key series is designed to help students to understand American school textbooks and to develop background knowledge in a wide variety of academic topics. This series also provides learners with the opportunity to enhance their reading comprehension skills and vocabulary, which will assist them when they take various English exams.

Reading Key <Volume 1-3> is
a three-book series designed for beginner to intermediate learners.

Reading Key <Volume 4-6> is
a three-book series designed for intermediate to high-intermediate learners.

Reading Key <Volume 7-9> is
a three-book series designed for high-intermediate learners.

Features

- A wide variety of topics that cover American school subjects
  helps learners expand their knowledge of academic topics through interdisciplinary studies
- Intensive practice for reading skill development
  helps learners prepare for various English exams
- Building vocabulary by school subjects and themed texts
  helps learners expand their vocabulary and reading skills in each subject
- Graphic organizers for each passage
  show the structure of the passage and help to build summary skills
- Captivating pictures and illustrations related to the topics
  help learners gain a broader understanding of the topics and key concepts

Table of Contents

Chapter 1
Social Studies • History and Geography

Chapter 2
Science

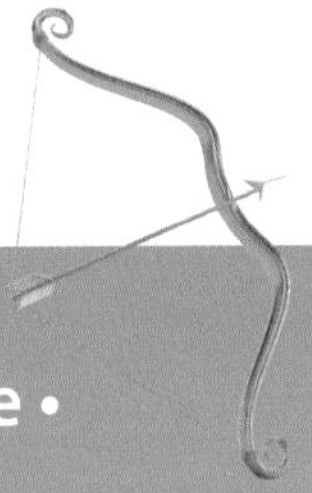

Syllabus Vol. 4

Subject	Topic & Area	Title
Social Studies ★ History and Geography	Citizenship	Moving to a New Community
	Citizenship	A Nation of Immigrants
	Economics	Earning, Spending, and Saving Money
	Economics	Our Needs and Wants
	World Geography	World Climate Regions
	World Geography	Extreme Weather Conditions
	Economics	Goods and Resources
	Economics	Goods and Services
	Government	American State and Local Governments
	Government	The Three Branches of Government
	Government	Laws and Rules
	Government	The Jury System
Science	A World of Plants	Kinds of Plants
	A World of Plants	How Do Plants Make Food?
	A World of Animals	Classifications of Animals
	A World of Animals	What Do Animals Need to Live and Grow?
	Food Chains	What Makes Up a Food Chain?
	Food Chains	Herbivores, Carnivores, and Omnivores
	Ecosystems	What Are Ecosystems?
	Ecosystems	Dinosaurs: Extinct but Still Popular
	The Weather and the Water Cycle	The Weather
	The Weather and the Water Cycle	The Water Cycle
	Earth's Resources	Rocks, Minerals, and Soil
	Earth's Resources	Fossils and Fossil Fuels
Mathematics	Geometry	Points, Lines, and Line Segments
	Geometry	Polygons
	Measurement	The U.S. Customary System and the Metric System
	Measurement	Measurement Word Problems
Language and Literature	Myths	Gods and Goddesses in Greek Myths
	Myths	Titans, Heroes, and Monsters in Greek Myths
	Myths	Same Gods, Different Names
	Myths	Cupid and Psyche
Visual Arts	Visual Arts	Architecture and Architects
	Visual Arts	Sculptures and Sculptors
Music	A World of Music	Elements of Music
	A World of Music	What's Your Vocal Range?

1

- Social Studies
- History and Geography

Unit 01

People Move From Place to Place

Moving to a New Community

Key Words

- entire
- grow up
- immigrant
- community
- look for
- opportunity
- improve
- seek
- freedom
- education
- obey

Some people live in the same places for their entire lives. They grow up, find jobs, and become old in the same city or town.

But other people move from place to place. They move to a nearby city or another state. Some people even move to different countries. We call these people immigrants.

So why do people move to a new community? Mostly, they are looking for opportunities to improve their lives. An opportunity is a chance for something better to happen. People often move to find a better life for themselves or their children. And some people even move to another country to seek freedom.

So what can people do in a new community? They can find new jobs, get a better education, or make friends. They can also try to become a part of it. They should obey the community's laws and respect other people so that the community becomes a good place to live.

✓ People move from place to place.

CANADA
UNITED STATES
WASHINGTON
MEXICO

My family moved to a new city because of my father's job.

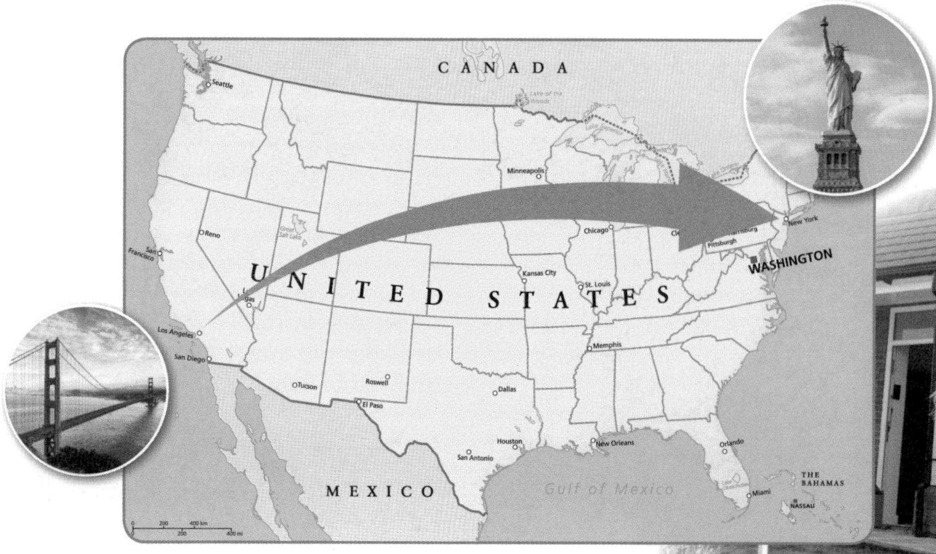

Main Idea and Details

1 What is the passage mainly about?

a. Why people move. b. Where people move. c. How people move.

2 People often move because they want better ____________.

a. families b. lives c. automobiles

3 What should people do in their new communities?

a. Invite their neighbors to their homes.
b. Obey the laws of their communities.
c. Teach people about their own cultures.

4 What does seek mean?

a. Look for. b. Create. c. Obey.

5 Complete the sentences.

a. Some people stay in the same city for their ____________ lives.
b. People move to get ____________________ to improve their lives.
c. Some people move to another country because they want ______________.

6 Complete the outline.

People Move From Place to Place

Where People Move	Why People Move	What People Do in a New Community
• Move to new cities or states • Move to new a ____________	• Want new jobs, better b ____________, or new friends • Seek c ____________	• Obey the d ________ and respect people in their new communities

Vocabulary Builder

Write the correct word and the meaning in Chinese.

1 ▸ a chance for something better to happen

____

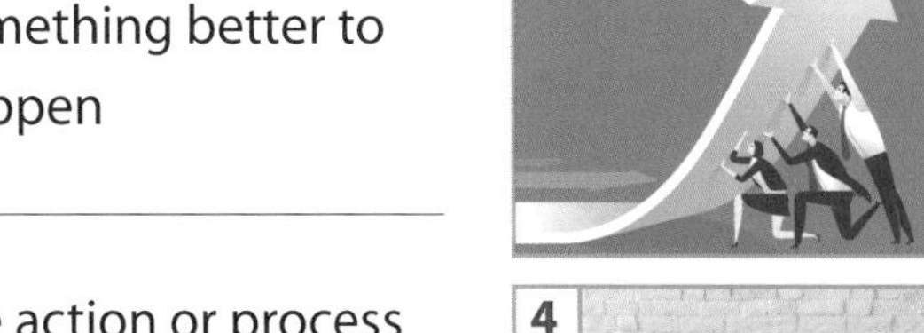

2 ▸ to become better or to make something better

____

3 ▸ the action or process of teaching someone especially in a school

____

4 ▸ a person who comes to a country to live there

____

Unit 02

People Move From Place to Place

A Nation of Immigrants

Key Words

- nation
- immigrant
- immigrate
- sail
- arrive at
- greet
- symbol
- get used to
- completely
- culture
- ethnic group

The United States is a nation of immigrants. People immigrate to the U.S. from all over the world.

In the early 1900s, many immigrants came from Europe. They sailed on ships across the Atlantic Ocean. They often arrived at Ellis Island in New York Harbor. In New York Harbor, the Statue of Liberty greeted them. For many immigrants, "Lady Liberty" was the first thing they saw in America. It was a symbol of freedom to these immigrants.

In the 1960s, many immigrants came from Asia. They often arrived at Angel Island in San Francisco Bay.

Moving to another country is not always easy. Immigrants have to get used to their new homes. They often have to start a completely new way of life. They have to learn about a new culture and find new jobs and homes. They need to learn a new language as well.

Some immigrants live with the same ethnic group. Ethnic neighbors can help them get used to their new country.

 Many people begin new lives in the United States.

immigrants in the early 1900s

Ellis Island in New York Harbor

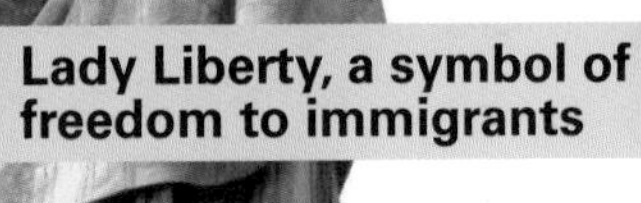

Lady Liberty, a symbol of freedom to immigrants

Angel Island in San Francisco Bay

Main Idea and Details

1 What is the main idea of the passage?

a. Most immigrants arrived at Ellis Island in New York.
b. Many immigrants have moved to America to live there.
c. There are a lot of Asian immigrants living in America.

2 Another name for the Statue of Liberty is "________________."

a. Mrs. Liberty **b.** Lady Liberty **c.** Aunt Freedom

3 Where is Angel Island?

a. In New York Harbor. **b.** In San Francisco Bay. **c.** Beside Ellis Island.

4 What does completely mean?

a. Slowly. **b.** Partially. **c.** Entirely.

5 According to the passage, which statement is true?

a. The Statue of Liberty is in San Francisco Bay.
b. Many immigrants leave America and go to other countries.
c. Many immigrants from Asia came to America in the 1960s.

6 Complete the outline.

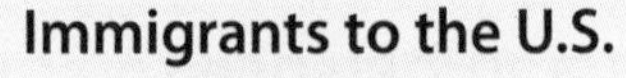

Immigrants to the U.S.

Early 1900s	1960s	In Their New Country
• Came from [a] __________ by ship • Arrived at Ellis Island in New York Harbor • Were greeted by the [b] ________ ____ ________	• Came from [c] ______ • Arrived at Angel Island in San Francisco Bay	• Must [d] ______ ______ to new homes • Learn a new culture and language • Find new jobs and homes

Vocabulary Builder

Write the correct word and the meaning in Chinese.

1 
the beliefs, customs, arts, etc., of a particular society

____

2 
to move to another country

____

3 
an object that represents a particular idea or quality

____

4 
a group of people who have the same ancestors and customs

____

Unit 03

Economics

Earning, Spending, and Saving Money

Key Words

- goods
- service
- get paid
- income
- earn
- earnings
- spend
- save
- budget
- spending
- savings
- control
- balance
- deposit

We use money to buy goods and services. When people work, they get paid. This money gives them an income. The money that people earn from working is called their earnings.

People often do two things with their income: They spend it or save it. People spend their money on various things. These include housing, food, transportation, clothes, and entertainment.

Most people try to spend less money than they earn. To do this, they often make a budget. A budget is a plan that shows income, spending, and savings. It is important to make a budget to control spending. With a budget, people can plan to buy something and balance their income and spending.

Many people save money to use later. If they do not save it, they will not have any money when they need it. People often deposit that money in a bank.

My Budget for July

Week	Income	Spending	Savings
Week 1	$10	$3 for pencil case	$7
Week 2	$10	$5 for Mom's birthday gift	$5
Week 3	$10	$3 for cap	$7
Week 4	$10	$2 for crayon	$8
Total	$40	$13	$27

Main Idea and Details

1 **What is the passage mainly about?**

a. The best way to save money.
b. How people can earn a lot of money.
c. What people do with their money.

2 **A ______________ helps people balance their spending and income.**

a. budget b. savings c. bank

3 **What are earnings?**

a. Money people spend. b. Money people make from working.
c. Money people save.

4 **What does deposit mean?**

a. Put. b. Spend. c. Make.

5 **Answer the questions.**

a. What do people use money for? ______________________________
b. What do people spend their money on? ______________________________
c. What do people often do with the money they save? ______________________________

6 **Complete the outline.**

People Earn, Spend, and Save Money

Earnings	Spending	Savings
• Get money from working • Can either spend it or [a] ______ it	• Use money for [b] __________, food, transportation, clothes, and entertainment • Try not to spend more money than they [c] ______	• Can use savings for later • Often deposit it in a [d] ______

Vocabulary Builder

Write the correct word and the meaning in Chinese.

1 
all the money people earn from working
____

2 
to adjust so that the amount of money available is more than or equal to the amount of money spent
____

3 
to put (money) in a bank account
____

4 
a plan that shows income, spending, and savings
____

Unit 04

Economics

Our Needs and Wants

Key Words

- go into debt
- category
- needs
- wants
- desire
- housing
- entertainment
- travel
- eat out
- socialize
- opportunity cost
- wise
- economic

People sometimes spend more money than they earn. When this happens, they go into debt. Most people try to avoid going into debt. So they spend their money carefully.

They divide the things they spend money on into two categories: needs and wants. Needs are things that people must have to live. Wants are things that people desire to have but do not need in order to live.

Needs are more important than wants. So people spend money on them first. What are some needs? Housing, food, and clothing are three important needs. Everyone needs a home to live in, food to eat, and clothes to wear.

What are some wants? Entertainment and traveling are wants. So are eating out and socializing.

People cannot buy everything that they want. They often have to make choices. They need to think about opportunity cost. In other words, if they spend money on one thing, they may not buy another. Opportunity cost can help people make wise economic choices.

Needs and Wants

needs

housing

clothing

food

wants

entertainment

traveling

eating out

socializing

Opportunity Cost

Opportunity cost is what you give up when you choose to buy one thing over another.

Main Idea and Details

1 What is the main idea of the passage?

a. Wants are more important than needs.
b. People have both wants and needs.
c. Entertainment and traveling are wants.

2 People can make wise economic choices by thinking about ____________.

a. their earnings b. opportunity cost c. socializing

3 What is a need?

a. Something a person must have.
b. Something a person thinks about.
c. Something a person wants to have.

4 What does wise mean?

a. Smart. b. Common. c. Poor.

5 Complete the sentences.

a. People that spend too much money may go into __________.
b. People must have __________ in order to live.
c. Eating out and socializing are __________.

6 Complete the outline.

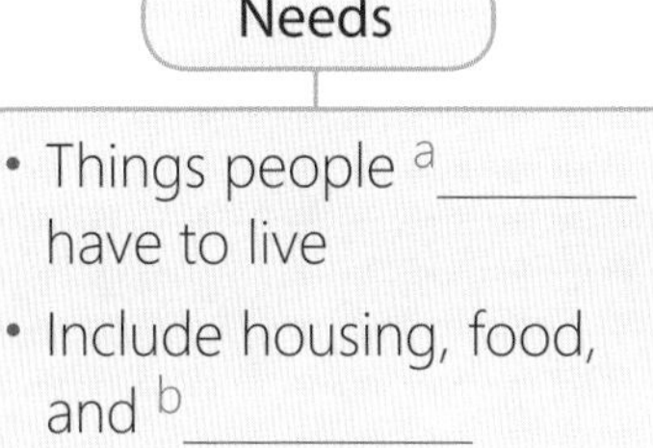

Spending Money

- Needs
  - Things people [a] ________ have to live
  - Include housing, food, and [b] ________
- Wants
  - Things people would like to have
  - Include [c] ____________, traveling, eating out, and socializing
- Opportunity Cost
  - Can help people make wise economic [d] ________

Vocabulary Builder

Write the correct word and the meaning in Chinese.

1 
the state of owing money to someone or something
____

2 
relating to money; not costing or spending much money
____

3 
to spend time with other people in a friendly way
____

4 
the value of something that is not chosen when you buy one thing over another
____

Vocabulary Review 1

A **Complete the sentences with the words below.**

freedom	grow up	chance	immigrants
Liberty	respect	ethnic	the world

1 Some people __________ __________, find jobs, and become old in the same city or town.

2 Some people even move to another country to seek __________.

3 An opportunity is a __________ for something better to happen.

4 They should obey the community's laws and __________ other people.

5 The United States is a nation of __________.

6 People immigrate to the U.S. from all over __________ __________.

7 For many immigrants, "Lady __________" was the first thing they saw in America.

8 __________ neighbors can help immigrants get used to their new country.

B **Complete the sentences with the words below.**

services	less	earnings	debt
spending	have	economic	desire

1 We use money to buy goods and __________.

2 The money that people earn from working is also called their __________.

3 Most people try to spend __________ money than they earn.

4 A budget is a plan that shows income, __________, and savings.

5 Most people try to avoid going into __________.

6 Needs are things that people must __________ to live.

7 Wants are things that people __________ to have but do not need in order to live.

8 Opportunity cost can help people make wise __________ choices.

C Write the correct word and the meaning in Chinese.

1 to try to find (someone or something)

____

2 a group of people who have the same ancestors and customs

____

3 to say hello to someone; to welcome

____

4 the amount of income that is not spent

____

5 things such as television and movies that give people pleasure

____

6 the houses, apartments, etc., in which people live

____

D Match each word with the correct definition and write the meaning in Chinese.

1 opportunity ______________ ☐

2 improve ______________ ☐

3 look for ______________ ☐

4 obey ______________ ☐

5 immigrate ______________ ☐

6 income ______________ ☐

7 spending ______________ ☐

8 budget ______________ ☐

9 desire ______________ ☐

10 opportunity cost ______________ ☐

a. to seek; to search for
b. to move to another country
c. to follow; to do what you are told to do
d. all the money people earn from working
e. a chance for something better to happen
f. to want or hope for something very much
g. to become better or to make something better
h. a plan that shows income, spending, and savings
i. the amount of income a person uses to buy goods and services
j. the value of something that is not chosen when you buy one thing over another

Unit 05

Living in Different Climates

World Climate Regions

Key Words

- diverse
- climate
- tropical
- temperate
- polar
- equator
- rain forest
- Antarctica
- experience
- distinct
- woodland
- prairie
- broadleaf
- needleleaf
- evergreen

Our planet is very large and diverse. So it has many different climates. Climate refers to the weather conditions in an area. There are three major climates. They are tropical, temperate, and polar climates.

Tropical climates have hot weather all year round. Tropical climates are found near the equator. Many times, these areas get lots of rain. There are often rain forests in places with tropical climates.

Polar climates have cold weather all year round. Polar climates are found in places like Antarctica and parts of Russia and Canada. They get a lot of snow and ice.

Most of the world has a temperate climate. It does not get too hot or too cold in temperate climates. These regions experience four distinct seasons. Temperate climates have many different areas. Sometimes, they have dry woodlands and prairies. Sometimes, they have broadleaf forests that lose their leaves in the fall. They also have needleleaf forests. These are forests of evergreens that keep their leaves during the winter.

World Climate Regions

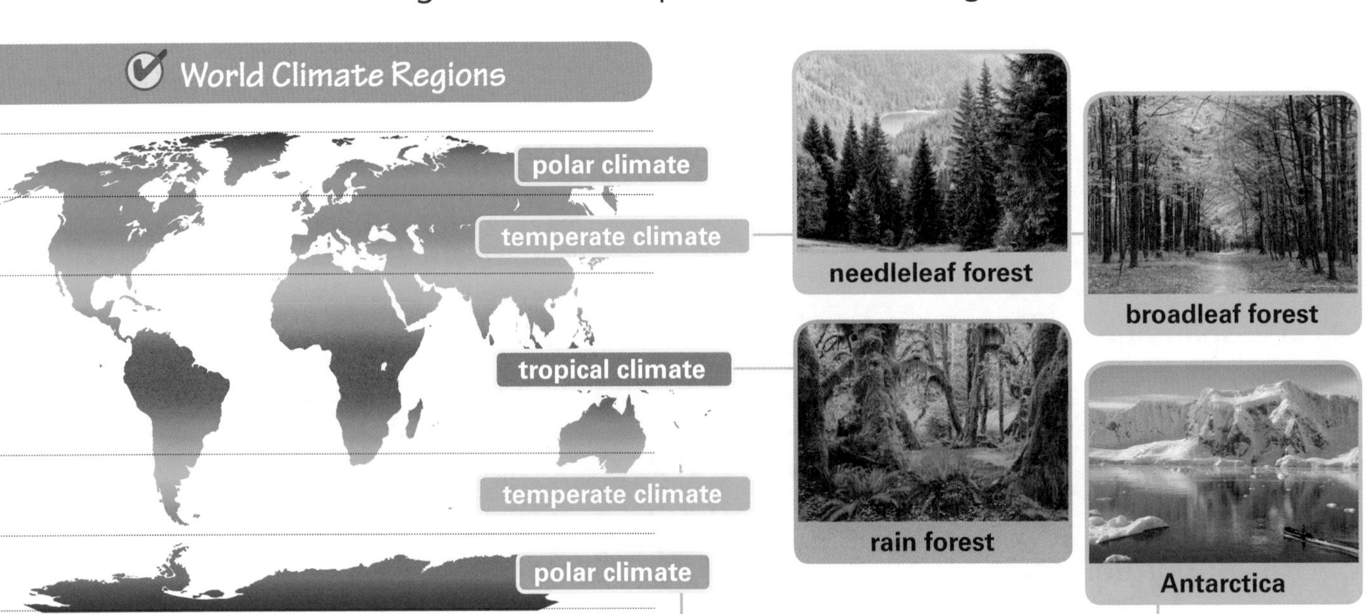

Main Idea and Details

1 **What is the main idea of the passage?**
- **a.** The weather in tropical climates can get very cold.
- **b.** Temperate climates have four distinct seasons.
- **c.** The earth has tropical, temperate, and polar climates.

2 **Some parts of ____________ have polar climates.**

a. Mexico **b.** England **c.** Russia

3 **What kind of climate is there near the equator?**

a. Tropical. **b.** Temperate. **c.** Polar.

4 **What does experience mean?**

a. Go through. **b.** Go up. **c.** Go around.

5 **According to the passage, which statement is true?**
- **a.** Rainforests are found in places with polar climates.
- **b.** Polar climates often get a lot of snow and ice.
- **c.** Evergreens are usually found in broadleaf forests.

6 **Complete the outline.**

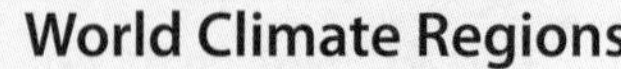

World Climate Regions

Tropical	Polar	Temperate
• Are hot all year • Are near the [a] ____________ • Often get lots of rain • May have rainforests	• Are cold [b] ____ ______ • Are in [c] ____________ and parts of Russia and Canada • Get lots of snow and ice	• Are not too hot or too cold • Have four distinct [d] ____________ • Have many different areas

Vocabulary Builder

Write the correct word and the meaning in Chinese.

1 

an imaginary line around the middle of the earth at an equal distance from both poles

____

2 

having relatively broad rather than needlelike leaves

____

3 

a climate that is not very hot or very cold

____

4 

a large open area of grassland

____

Living in Different Climates

Extreme Weather Conditions

Key Words

- violent
- extreme
- blizzard
- tropical storm
- thunder
- lightning
- hurricane
- typhoon
- tornado
- twister
- damage
- flood
- drought
- natural hazard
- monsoon

We usually experience normal weather conditions. But, sometimes the weather may become violent. In these cases, people experience extreme forms of weather.

Extreme weather can be dangerous. There are many types of extreme weather.

In winter, sometimes the snow falls so hard that it is impossible to see anything except for the color white. This is a blizzard. Blizzards can drop huge amounts of snow at one time.

Tropical storms have high winds, heavy rain, thunder, and lightning. Hurricanes and typhoons are two types of these storms. Tornadoes are another kind of storm. These are twisters that have winds that blow extremely quickly. They can cause a lot of damage.

Floods and droughts are other examples of natural hazards. Tropical storms and heavy monsoon rains often cause floods. Drought areas get no rain for a long time. The plants there die, and the soil blows away.

Extreme Weather

blizzard

tropical storm

tornado

flood

drought

Main Idea and Details

1 What is the passage mainly about?

a. Extreme types of weather.

b. Hurricanes and tornadoes.

c. How many people die in extreme weather.

2 A place that gets no rain for a long time is experiencing a ___________.

a. tornado b. flood c. drought

3 What falls during a blizzard?

a. Snow. b. Rain. c. Ice.

4 What does forms mean?

a. Situations. b. Types. c. Hazards.

5 Answer the questions.

a. What are hurricanes and typhoons? ______________________

b. What can cause a flood? ______________________

____

c. What is the name of a storm that has a twister? ______________________

6 Complete the outline.

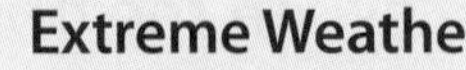

Extreme Weather

- Blizzards
  - Heavy [a] ________
  - Can only see white during them
- Tropical Storms
  - Hurricanes and [b] ________
  - Have high winds, heavy rain, thunder, and [c] ________
  - Can cause floods
- Other Types of Weather
  - Tornadoes = [d] ________ with fast-blowing winds
  - Droughts = periods of no rain

Vocabulary Builder

Write the correct word and the meaning in Chinese.

1 
a severe snowstorm that goes on for a long time ________

2 
a naturally occurring threat that has a negative effect on people or the environment ________

3 
a period of no rain ________

4 
a storm with very strong winds that occurs especially in the western part of the Atlantic Ocean ________

Unit 07

Using Resources

Goods and Resources

Key Words

- natural resource
- produce
- goods
- pump
- fuel
- mineral
- renewable resource
- nonrenewable resource
- solar power
- wind power
- replace
- forever
- limited
- conserve

There are many kinds of natural resources on the earth. People use natural resources to produce goods.

Trees are used to build our homes and buildings. Oil that is pumped from the ground is made into fuel and other products we use every day. Minerals, such as gold and salt, are also very important natural resources.

We can divide the earth's resources into renewable and nonrenewable resources.

Renewable resources can be used again and again. Water, soil, and trees are renewable resources. Also, solar power and wind power are renewable resources. They can be replaced within a short time.

Nonrenewable resources are the opposite. We can only use them once, and then they are gone forever. Many energy resources, such as oil, coal, and natural gas, are nonrenewable resources. They are limited in supply and cannot be replaced easily.

We must conserve our natural resources so that we do not run out of them.

Main Idea and Details

1 What is the passage mainly about?

a. Minerals and goods.
b. Solar power and wind power.
c. Renewable and nonrenewable resources.

2 Gold and salt are two kinds of ______________.

a. fuels b. renewable resources c. minerals

3 Which of the following are nonrenewable resources?

a. Solar power. b. Natural gas. c. Water.

4 What does replaced mean?

a. Restored. b. Constructed. c. Supplied.

5 Complete the sentences.

a. We can ______________ oil from the ground to use as fuel.
b. Some ______________ resources are water, soil, and trees.
c. There is a ______________ supply of nonrenewable resources.

6 Complete the outline.

Natural Resources

Renewable	Nonrenewable
• Can be used [a] ________	• Can only be used [c] ________
• Water, soil, and trees	• Oil, coal, and natural gas
• Solar power and [b] ________ ________	• A limited supply
• Can be replaced within a short time	• Cannot be [d] ________ easily

Vocabulary Builder

Write the correct word and the meaning in Chinese.

1

a resource that can be used again
____

2

power derived from wind
____

3

a substance (such as gold and salt) that is naturally formed under the ground
____

4

to use carefully to avoid waste; to preserve
____

Unit 08

Using Resources

Goods and Services

Key Words

- factory
- goods
- furniture
- crop
- customer
- producer
- purchase
- consumer
- travel agent
- product
- profit
- cost

Companies and factories make goods such as cars, computers, and furniture. Farmers grow crops in soil. Then, they sell these goods to customers.

Goods are things made or grown for sale. Vegetables, books, and ice cream are all goods. Any person or company that makes goods is a producer. Producers try to sell their goods to people. We call the people who purchase goods consumers.

Some people provide services for others. Waiters, cooks, travel agents, and bus and taxi drivers all have service jobs. Together, goods and services are called products.

Most businesses make goods and provide services to make a profit. Profit is the income a business has left after all its costs are paid. So, how do businesses make a profit? They can earn a profit if they sell their products at higher prices than it costs to provide them.

Businesses make profits by selling or providing products.

▸ Producer

▸ Make and sell goods
▸ Provide services

▸ Buy goods or services

▸ Consumer

Businesses earn profits

Main Idea and Details

1 **What is the passage mainly about?**

a. How to make a profit.

b. Workers in the service industry.

c. Goods and services being sold to make a profit.

2 **A person who makes any kind of goods is a ______________.**

a. consumer　　b. producer　　c. service worker

3 **What is the money a business earns called?**

a. Profit.　　b. Product.　　c. Service.

4 **What does purchase mean?**

a. Consume.　　b. Pay.　　c. Buy.

5 **According to the passage, which statement is true?**

a. Waiters and chefs are consumers.

b. Books and ice cream are services.

c. Most businesses try to earn a profit.

6 **Complete the outline.**

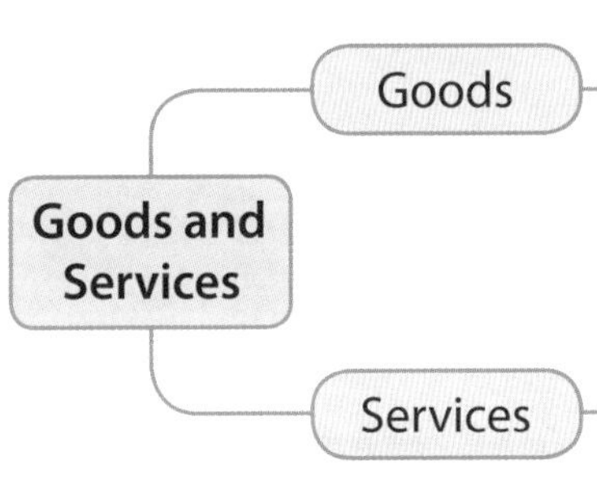

Goods:
- Things made or grown for [a] ________
- Are made by producers
- Are sold to [b] ______________

Services:
- Are things that people provide for others
- Include waiters, cooks, [c] __________ __________, and bus and taxi drivers

- Are sold to make a profit
- Profit = money left over after [d] ________ are paid

Vocabulary Builder

Write the correct word and the meaning in Chinese.

1 
to buy something

____

2 
plants such as corn and wheat that are grown for food

____

3 
a person or company that grows food or makes goods to be sold

____

4 
money left over after costs are paid

____

Vocabulary Review 2

A **Complete the sentences with the words below.**

diverse	hazards	normal	at one time
equator	polar	lightning	temperate

1 Our planet is very large and ___________.

2 Tropical climates are found near the ___________.

3 _________ climates have cold weather all year round.

4 Most of the world has a ___________ climate.

5 We usually experience ___________ weather conditions.

6 Blizzards can drop huge amounts of snow ______ ________ ________.

7 Tropical storms have high winds, heavy rain, thunder, and ___________.

8 Floods and droughts are other examples of natural ___________.

B **Complete the sentences with the words below.**

renewable	goods	resources	profit
energy	costs	wind power	products

1 People use natural ___________ to produce goods.

2 We can divide the earth's resources into ___________ and nonrenewable resources.

3 Solar power and _________ _________ are renewable resources.

4 Many ___________ resources, such as oil, coal, and natural gas, are nonrenewable resources.

5 Any person or company that makes ___________ is a producer.

6 Together, goods and services are called ___________.

7 Most businesses make goods and provide services to make a ___________.

8 Profit is the income a business has left after all its ___________ are paid.

C Write the correct word and the meaning in Chinese.

1 a forest of evergreens that has trees with small, needlelike leaves ______________

2 a period of heavy rain in India and Southeast Asia ______________

3 a resource that cannot be used again ______________

4 energy from the sun that is converted into thermal or electrical energy ______________

5 things made or grown for sale ______________

6 plants such as corn and wheat that are grown for food ______________

D Match each word with the correct definition and write the meaning in Chinese.

1 climate ______________ ☐
2 temperate climate ______________ ☐
3 distinct ______________ ☐
4 extreme ______________ ☐
5 natural hazard ______________ ☐
6 monsoon ______________ ☐
7 replace ______________ ☐
8 conserve ______________ ☐
9 consumer ______________ ☐
10 profit ______________ ☐

a. a person who buys goods
b. clearly different or separate
c. to take the place of; to restore
d. money left over after costs are paid
e. the weather conditions in an area
f. very great in degree; very unusual
g. to use carefully to avoid waste; to preserve
h. a climate that is not very hot or very cold
i. the season when it rains a lot in Southern Asia
j. a naturally occurring threat that has a negative effect on people or the environment

Unit 09

The Government

American State and Local Governments

Key Words

- government
- local
- state
- national
- operate
- be responsible for
- govern
- federal government
- take care of
- be based
- state capital
- enforce
- in charge of
- national security
- infrastructure
- interstate

The United States has several types of government. They include local, state, and national governments.

Local governments operate in towns, cities, and counties. State governments are responsible for governing their states. And the national, or federal, government is responsible for the entire country.

Local governments provide services for the people in their communities. Mostly, they take care of schools, fire departments, and police departments.

State governments govern an entire state. They are based in the state capital. For example, Boston, Massachusetts, and Atlanta, Georgia, are the capitals of their states. The state government is responsible for enforcing the state's laws.

The national government is based in Washington, D.C. Most importantly, the national government is responsible for keeping all Americans safe. It is in charge of national security. But the government does other things, too. It makes and enforces the country's laws. And it builds infrastructure such as interstates and highways.

Local governments provide community services.

State governments are based in the state capital.

The national government is in charge of national security.

Main Idea and Details

1 What is the main idea of the passage?

a. Each state has its own capital.
b. There are several types of government.
c. The federal government takes care of national security.

2 The capital of Georgia is ______________.

a. Washington, D.C. b. Boston c. Atlanta

3 Where do local governments operate?

a. In a state. b. In a city. c. In a country.

4 What does enforcing mean?

a. Electing. b. Making. c. Carrying out.

5 Answer the questions.

a. What is the national government responsible for? ______________
b. What are most local governments responsible for? ______________
c. Where is the U.S. national government based? ______________

6 Complete the outline.

Local
- Operate in towns, cities, and counties
- Are [a] __________ for schools, fire departments, and police departments

State
- Govern an entire state
- Are [b] __________ in state capitals
- Enforce the state's laws

National
- Is responsible for the entire country
- Is based in Washington, D.C.
- Is in [c] __________ of national security
- Makes and [d] __________ laws
- Builds infrastructure

Vocabulary Builder

Write the correct word and the meaning in Chinese.

1 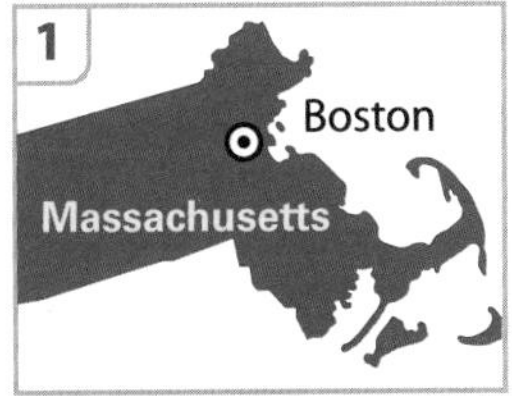

the capital city of a political subdivision of a country ______________

2 

to make sure that a law or rule is obeyed by people ______________

3 

to officially control or run a county, state, etc. ______________

4 

the basic structures needed for a country or area to function properly ______________

Unit 10

The Government

The Three Branches of Government

Key Words

- Constitution
- separate
- branch
- executive
- legislative
- judicial
- duty
- carry out
- Congress
- the Senate
- the House of Representatives
- role
- court

The Constitution is the highest law of the USA. It divides the government into three separate branches. They are the executive, legislative, and judicial branches. Each branch has different duties and responsibilities.

The head of the executive branch is the president. The president enforces the country's laws. The president cannot do this alone. So many people work for him. The FBI, CIA, and Department of Defense are all part of the executive branch. Together, they carry out the nation's laws.

The legislative branch is Congress. Congress is divided into two houses. The upper house is the Senate, and the lower house is the House of Representatives. Congress's role is to make the country's laws.

The judicial branch is the court system. The Supreme Court is the nation's highest court. But there are many lower courts all throughout the country. These courts determine if people have broken the law or not.

The American government is divided into three branches.

▲ The executive branch enforces laws.

▲ The legislative branch makes laws.

▲ The judicial branch determines if laws have been broken.

Main Idea and Details

1 What is the passage mainly about?

a. The two houses of Congress.
b. The three branches of government.
c. The FBI, CIA, and Department of Defense.

2 The Supreme Court is part of the ______________.

a. executive branch
b. judicial branch
c. legislative branch

3 Who is the head of the executive branch?

a. The President.
b. The Senate.
c. The House of Representatives.

4 What does divides mean?

a. Splits.
b. Chooses.
c. Determines.

5 Complete the sentences.

a. The highest law in the USA is the ______________.
b. The ______________ branch carries out the nation's laws.
c. The ______________ system makes up the judicial branch.

6 Complete the outline.

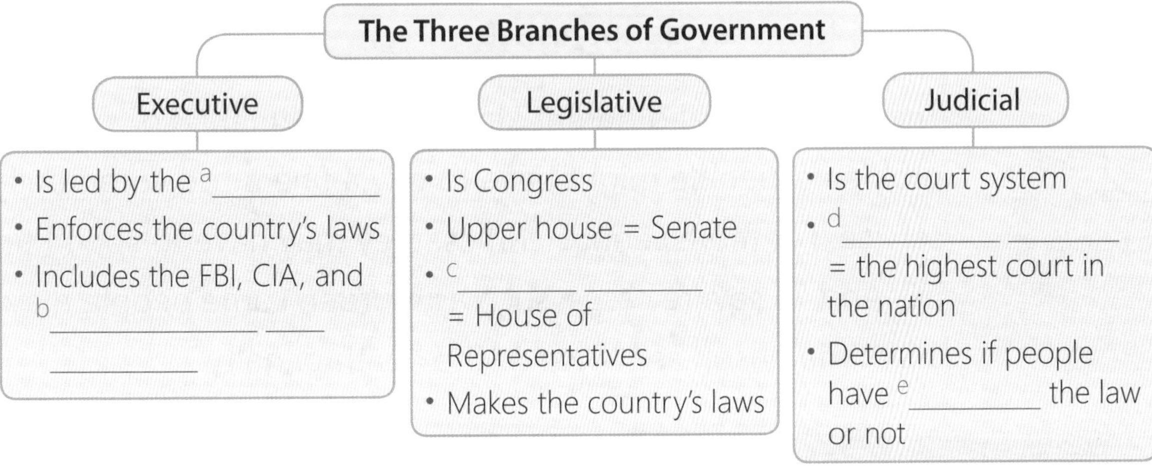

Vocabulary Builder

Write the correct word and the meaning in Chinese.

1 
the highest law of the USA
____

2 
the upper house of Congress in the U.S.
____

3 
the lower house of Congress in the U.S.
____

4 
a place where trials take place and legal cases are decided
____

Unit 11 Laws and Rules

Key Words

- citizen
- freedom of the press
- go to court
- guilty
- get punished
- punishment
- fine
- community service
- crime
- jail
- murder
- lifetime prison sentence
- death penalty

Every citizen has many rights and responsibilities.

The Constitution explains the rights that all Americans have. For example, Americans have the right to freedom of speech, religion, and the press. They also have many other rights.

However, Americans also have many responsibilities. For instance, they have to obey all of the laws in the country. There are many federal laws. There are also state laws and local laws.

Unfortunately, people sometimes break the law. When people break the law, they must often go to court. If they are found guilty, they may get punished.

There are several different kinds of punishment. For small problems, people might have to pay a fine or do community service. For more serious crimes, they may have to spend time in jail. And, in severe cases, such as murder, some people may get a lifetime prison sentence or the death penalty.

Americans have many rights and responsibilities.

freedom of speech

freedom of religion

freedom of the press

obeying laws

Kinds of Punishment

fine

community service

jail term

death penalty

Main Idea and Details

1 What is the main idea of the passage?

a. Citizens have both rights and responsibilities.
b. People who break the law may go to jail.
c. It is important to obey all federal laws.

2 A person who commits ______________ may get the death penalty.

a. robbery   b. murder   c. a traffic violation

3 Which right do American citizens have?

a. Freedom of government.
b. Freedom of speech.
c. Freedom of driving.

4 What does responsibilities mean?

a. Chores.   b. Jobs.   c. Duties.

5 According to the passage, which statement is true?

a. People should always obey the law.
b. People who break the law go to the press.
c. The death penalty is a punishment for a small crime.

6 Complete the outline.

Rights

- Freedom of speech, a__________, and the press
- Many other rights

Responsibilities

- Must obey all of the country's laws
- b________ the law → go to court
- Small problem → pay a c______ or do community service
- Big problem → spend time in jail or get the death d__________

Vocabulary Builder

Write the correct word and the meaning in Chinese.

1

▸ money that you have to pay as a type of punishment

____

2

▸ the right of newspapers to report news without being controlled by the government

____

3
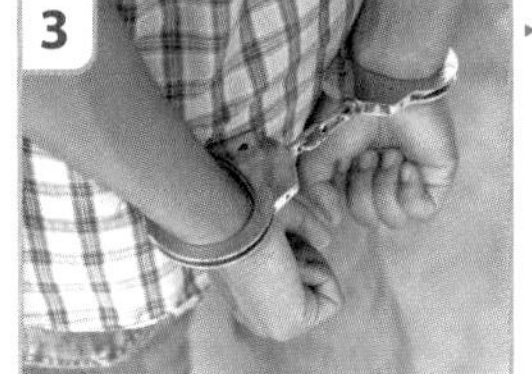
▸ having committed a crime

____

4

▸ the punishment of being sent to prison for the rest of one's life

____

The Jury System

Key Words

- trial
- jury
- justice system
- housewife
- grand jury
- petit jury
- evidence
- vote against
- criminal case
- prosecutor
- defendant
- judge
- proceed
- verdict

The Constitution gives all Americans the right to a trial by jury. In the United States, jury trials are an important part of the justice system.

A jury is made up of regular citizens. It can be formed of anyone, such as businessmen, housewives, doctors, or college students.

There are two kinds of juries: a grand jury and a petit jury.

Grand juries usually have 12 to 23 members. They decide if there is enough evidence to have a trial. If there is enough evidence, they vote to have a trial. If there is not enough evidence, they vote against having a trial. Then, there will be no trial.

Petit juries decide actual criminal cases. They usually have 12 members. The petit jury listens to the prosecutor and defendant during the trial. Each trial has a judge, too. The judge helps the case proceed smoothly. At the end of the trial, the jury decides on a verdict. It decides if the defendant is guilty or not guilty.

Grand Jury and Petit Jury

The grand jury decides if there is enough evidence to have a trial.

The petit jury gives a verdict for actual criminal cases.

Main Idea and Details

1 What is the passage mainly about?

a. Two kinds of juries. b. Criminal cases. c. Grand juries.

2 A petit jury usually has ________ members.

a. 2 b. 12 c. 23

3 What does a grand jury do?

a. It decides criminal cases.

b. It listens to the prosecutor and defendant.

c. It decides if there is enough evidence for a trial.

4 What does evidence mean?

a. Paper. b. Police. c. Proof.

5 Complete the sentences.

a. Regular ____________ make up a jury.

b. When there is not enough evidence, there will be no __________.

c. The ____________ helps a case proceed smoothly.

6 Complete the outline.

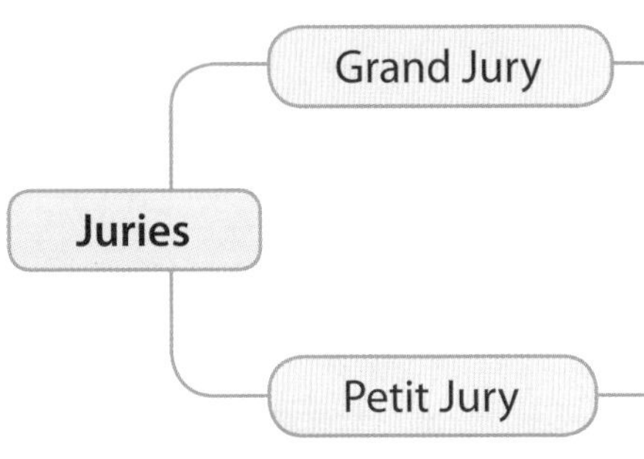

Grand Jury:
- Has 12 to 23 members
- Decides if there is enough [a] __________ for a case
- Enough evidence = have a trial
- Not enough evidence = no [b] _____

Petit Jury:
- Has 12 members
- Decides [c] __________ cases
- Listens to the prosecutor and [d] __________
- Decides on a verdict

Vocabulary Builder

Write the correct word and the meaning in Chinese.

1 
a group of people who decide actual criminal cases

____

2 
the process of examining a case in a court of law and deciding whether someone is guilty or not

____

3 
a person who acts as a lawyer against the defendant

____

4 
someone who has been accused of a crime and is on trial

____

Vocabulary Review 3

A **Complete the sentences with the words below.**

communities	governments	Congress's	judicial
keeping	executive	govern	branches

1 The United States has local, state, and national ______________.

2 Local governments provide services for the people in their ______________.

3 State governments __________ an entire state.

4 The national government is responsible for __________ all Americans safe.

5 The Constitution divides the government into three separate __________.

6 The FBI, CIA, and Department of Defense are all part of the __________ branch.

7 __________ role is to make the country's laws.

8 The __________ branch is the court system.

B **Complete the sentences with the words below.**

Constitution	court	evidence	serious
community service	right	regular	trial

1 Americans have the ________ to freedom of speech, religion, and the press.

2 When people break the law, they must often go to ________.

3 For small problems, people might have to pay a fine or do ______________ __________.

4 For more __________ crimes, they may have to spend time in jail.

5 The ______________ gives all Americans the right to a trial by jury.

6 A jury is made up of __________ citizens.

7 Grand juries decide if there is enough ____________ to have a trial.

8 At the end of the ________, the jury decides on a verdict.

C Write the correct word and the meaning in Chinese.

1

the national government

____

2

the basic structures needed for a country or area to function properly

____

3

the branch that determines if laws have been broken

____

4

the crime of killing someone deliberately

____

5

a group of people who decide actual criminal cases

____

6

an official judgment made in a court about whether someone is guilty of a crime

____

D Match each word with the correct definition and write the meaning in Chinese.

1 executive branch ______________ ☐

2 be responsible for ______________ ☐

3 govern ______________ ☐

4 the Senate ______________ ☐

5 the House of Representatives ______________ ☐

6 fine ______________ ☐

7 guilty ______________ ☐

8 jail ______________ ☐

9 prosecutor ______________ ☐

10 verdict ______________ ☐

a. having committed a crime
b. to be in charge of; to take care of
c. the lower house of Congress in the U.S.
d. the upper house of Congress in the U.S.
e. the branch that enforces the country's laws
f. to officially control or run a county, state, etc.
g. a person who acts as a lawyer against the defendant
h. money that you have to pay as a type of punishment
i. the decision that is given by the jury at the end of a trial
j. a place where someone is sent to be punished for a crime

Wrap-Up Test 1

A Write the correct word for each sentence.

immigrate	nonrenewable	savings	temperate	local
seek	in order to	floods	businesses	justice

1 Some people move to another country to ________ freedom.
2 People ______________ to the U.S. from all over the world.
3 A budget is a plan that shows income, spending, and ___________.
4 Wants are things that people desire to have but do not need ___ _______ ___ live.
5 Most of the world has a ______________ climate.
6 __________ and droughts are other examples of natural hazards.
7 We can divide the earth's resources into renewable and __________________ resources.
8 Most ______________ make goods and provide services to make a profit.
9 The United States has _________, state, and national governments.
10 In the United States, jury trials are an important part of the __________ system.

B Write the meanings of the words in Chinese.

1 immigrant ________________
2 ethnic group ________________
3 greet ________________
4 entertainment ________________
5 socialize ________________
6 improve ________________
7 look for ________________
8 immigrate ________________
9 budget ________________
10 opportunity cost ________________
11 needleleaf forest ________________
12 drought ________________
13 goods ________________
14 crops ________________
15 polar climate ________________
16 distinct ________________
17 extreme ________________
18 natural hazard ________________
19 monsoon ________________
20 replace ________________
21 judicial branch ________________
22 executive branch ________________
23 legislative branch ________________
24 Congress ________________
25 freedom of speech ________________
26 fine ________________
27 community service ________________
28 evidence ________________
29 verdict ________________
30 infrastructure ________________

2

Science

Unit 13

A World of Plants

Kinds of Plants

Key Words

- species
- flowering plant
- conifer
- produce
- seed
- reproduce
- cone
- pine tree
- fir tree
- spruce tree
- evergreen tree
- needle
- deciduous tree
- broad leaf

There are many species of plants. However, scientists divide them into two main groups. These are flowering plants and conifers.

The main difference between them is how they produce their seeds. A plant's seeds are what let it reproduce.

Flowering plants have flowers and produce seeds in flowers. Most plants are flowering plants. They include peas, strawberries, cherries, and roses.

Conifers do not have flowers. Instead, they produce their seeds in cones. Pine trees, fir trees, and spruce trees are conifers.

Many conifers are evergreen trees. Evergreen trees have needles instead of leaves and stay green all year long.

While most conifers have needles for leaves, the majority of trees are deciduous trees. Deciduous trees have broad leaves that usually change color in the fall. Also, they drop their leaves in winter. In spring, the leaves grow back again.

Main Idea and Details

1 **What is the main idea of the passage?**

a. Deciduous trees drop their leaves in winters.
b. There are two major kinds of plants.
c. Conifers have seeds in cones.

2 **Peas, strawberries, cherries, and roses are ____________.**

a. conifers b. deciduous trees c. flowering plants

3 **Where are the seeds in flowering plants?**

a. In their leaves. b. In their flowers. c. In their cones.

4 **What does produce mean?**

a. Divide. b. Drop. c. Make.

5 **Complete the sentences.**

a. Plants' ____________ let them reproduce.
b. Many conifers are evergreen trees that have ____________.
c. The leaves of deciduous trees change color in the ____________.

6 **Complete the outline.**

Kinds of Plants

Flowering Plants
- Have flowers
- Produce seeds in [a] ____________
- Include peas, strawberries, cherries, and roses

Conifers
- Produce seeds inside of [b] ____________
- Include [c] ________ ________, fir trees, and spruce trees
- Are often evergreen trees
- Have needles

Deciduous Trees
- Are the majority of trees
- Have [d] ________ leaves that change color in the fall
- Drop leaves in winter

Vocabulary Builder

Write the correct word and the meaning in Chinese.

1 
a leaf that is shaped like a very thin stick
____

2 
trees that have broad leaves that drop in winter
____

3 
trees that have needles and stay green all year long
____

4 
the fruit of a pine tree or other evergreen plant and contains many seeds
____

Unit 14

A World of Plants

How Do Plants Make Food?

Key Words

- process
- photosynthesis
- substance
- chlorophyll
- chloroplast
- absorb
- carbon dioxide
- occur
- take in
- give off
- oxygen
- breathe
- stay alive

All living things need energy to live. Animals eat food to get energy. But plants make their own food. They do this in a process called photosynthesis.

Plants use sunlight in order to make their food. Leaves are the main food-making part of a plant.

A leaf is green because it has a substance called chlorophyll. Chlorophyll is found in chloroplasts, which are where a plant makes its food.

First, when the sun shines on a leaf, the chlorophyll absorbs sunlight. Then, the chloroplasts use carbon dioxide, water, and the sun's energy to make sugar. The sugar is food for the plant. This process is photosynthesis.

As photosynthesis occurs, the plant takes in carbon dioxide from the air. At the same time, the plant gives off oxygen into the air. This is what people breathe. All animals must breathe in oxygen to stay alive. So, thanks to plants, people and animals can live, too.

The Process of Photosynthesis

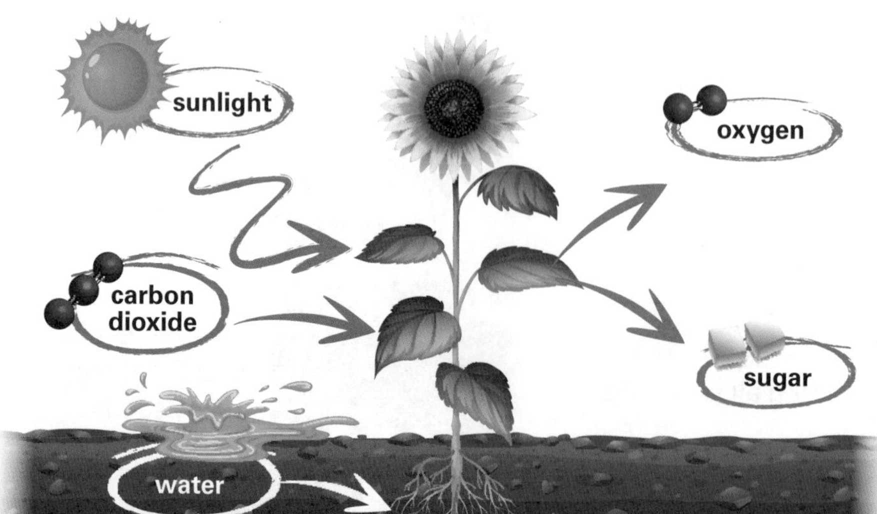

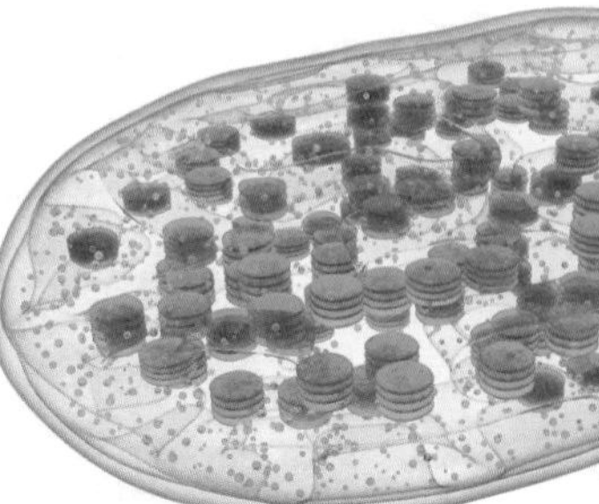

chloroplast

Main Idea and Details

1 What is the passage mainly about?

a. What chlorophyll does.
b. What carbon dioxide is.
c. How photosynthesis occurs.

2 Plants' leaves are green because of ______________.

a. chlorophyll　b. chloroplasts　c. photosynthesis

3 What does a plant take in from the air?

a. Nitrogen.　b. Oxygen.　c. Carbon dioxide.

4 What does substance mean?

a. Food.　b. Material.　c. Air.

5 According to the passage, which statement is true?

a. Plants need oxygen to stay alive.
b. Plants can absorb sugar from the ground.
c. Chloroplasts are where plants do photosynthesis.

6 Complete the outline.

How Plants Make Food

Plants
- Have green leaves
- Leaves have a ______________.
- Chlorophyll is located in b ______________.

Photosynthesis
- Sun shines on leaf.
- Chlorophyll c ____________ sunlight.
- Chloroplasts use carbon dioxide + water + sunlight → d __________ + oxygen.

Vocabulary Builder

Write the correct word and the meaning in Chinese.

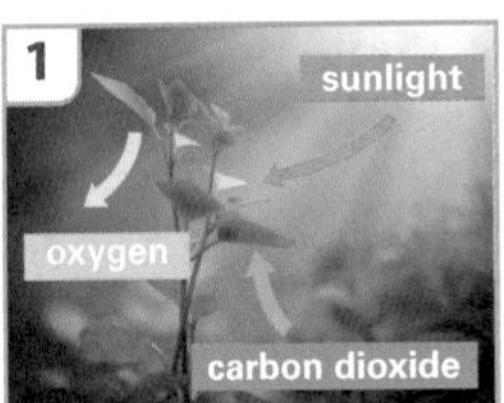

the process plants use to make food

____

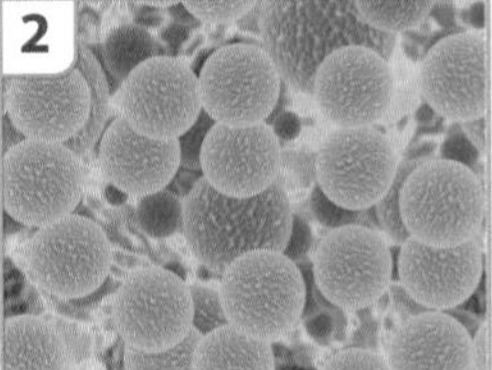

the green substance in a leaf

____

to take air into your lungs through your nose or mouth and let it out again

____

a gas that is produced when people and animals breathe out

____

Unit 15

A World of Animals

Classifications of Animals

Key Words

- group
- trait
- classify
- backbone
- vertebrate
- amphibian
- invertebrate
- flatworm
- sponge
- warm-blooded
- cold-blooded
- regulate
- surrounding
- soak up

Animals can be grouped according to their traits. One way to classify animals is by whether or not they have backbones.

An animal with a backbone is called a vertebrate. All mammals, birds, reptiles, fish, and amphibians are vertebrates.

An animal without a backbone is called an invertebrate. Invertebrates include insects, flatworms, sponges, shrimp, and lobsters.

All vertebrates can be further divided into two classes: warm-blooded animals and cold-blooded animals.

Warm-blooded animals can regulate their body temperatures. So, even if it is very cold or very hot outside, their bodies stay the same temperature. Mammals and birds are warm-blooded.

Cold-blooded animals need the sun to warm their bodies. So their body temperatures can change with the surrounding temperature. These animals often rest in the sun for hours to soak up heat. Reptiles, fish, and amphibians are cold-blooded.

Animals can be classified according to their traits.

Main Idea and Details

1 What is the passage mainly about?

a. Some species of vertebrates.
b. The different classifications of animals.
c. Warm-blooded and cold-blooded animals.

2 A flatworm is ____________________.

a. a warm-blooded animal b. an invertebrate c. a vertebrate

3 What can warm-blooded animals do?

a. Live without backbones.
b. Use the sun to heat themselves.
c. Regulate their body temperatures.

4 What does backbones mean?

a. Brains. b. Legs. c. Spines.

5 According to the passage, which statement is true?

a. Which animals are vertebrates? ____________________
b. Which animals are invertebrates? ____________________
c. Which animals are warm-blooded? ____________________

6 Complete the outline.

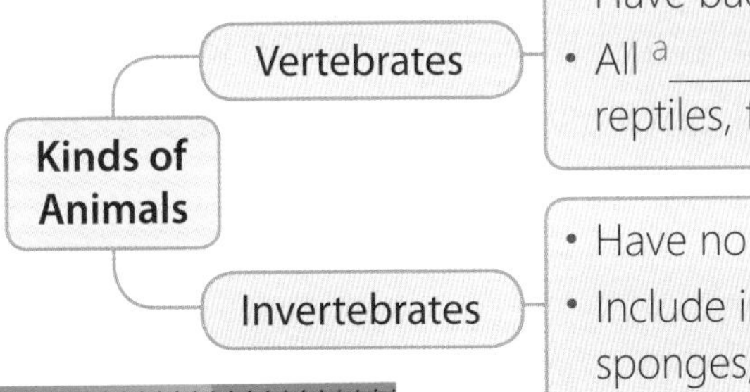

Kinds of Animals
- Vertebrates
  - Have backbones
  - All [a] __________, birds, reptiles, fish, and amphibians
    - [c] __________ animals = mammals and birds
    - Can regulate their body temperatures
    - [d] __________ animals = reptiles, fish, and amphibians
    - Need the [e] ______ to warm their bodies
- Invertebrates
  - Have no [b] __________
  - Include insects, flatworms, sponges, shrimp, and lobsters

Vocabulary Builder

Write the correct word and the meaning in Chinese.

1

a particular characteristic or quality

____

2

an animal that can live both on land and in water

____

3

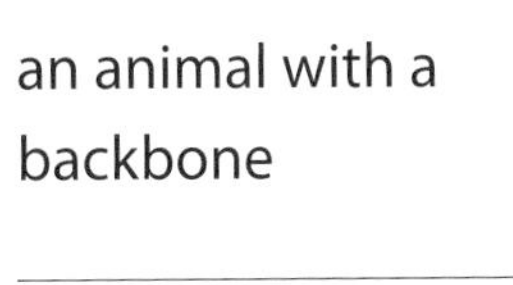

an animal with a backbone

____

4

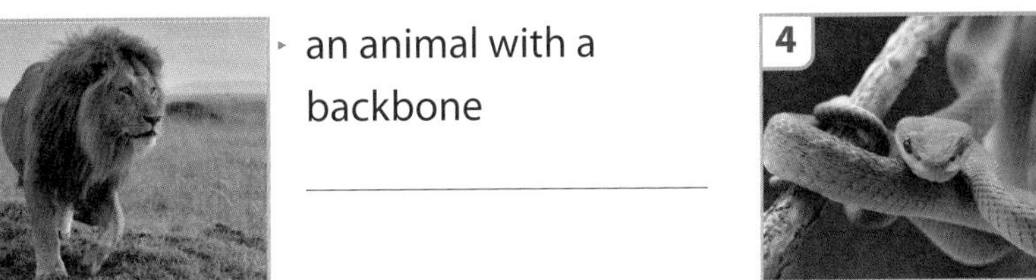

having a body temperature that is similar to the temperature of the environment

____

Unit 16

A World of Animals

What Do Animals Need to Live and Grow?

Key Words

- basic needs
- shelter
- stay alive
- run
- gill
- respond to
- environment
- survive
- migrate
- hibernate

All animals have basic needs to live and grow. They all need food, water, air, and shelter.

All animals need food and water to stay alive. Food and water give an animal energy. Like fuel runs a machine, all animals need energy to work. As an animal grows, it needs more food and water.

All animals need oxygen to breathe. How do animals get oxygen? Animals that live on land take in oxygen through their lungs. But fish and some water animals do not have lungs. Instead, they breathe with gills to take in oxygen from water.

All animals need a shelter—a place to live. This shelter keeps them safe from the weather and from other animals.

Animals also respond to changes in their environment to survive. When the weather gets colder, some animals migrate to warmer places. Some animals find places to hibernate. Cold-blooded animals lie in the sunlight to warm their bodies.

Basic Needs for All Animals

Main Idea and Details

1 What is the main idea of the passage?

a. Every animal has some needs in order to live.
b. Fish have gills, but land animals have lungs.
c. Animals need shelter to be safe from other animals.

2 Animals with lungs live ______________.

a. on land b. in the air c. in the water

3 What is a shelter?

a. A place to live. b. Air to breathe. c. Food to eat.

4 What does runs mean?

a. Organizes. b. Operates. c. Orders.

5 Complete the sentences.

a. Animals get energy from food and ____________.
b. Shelter protects animals from the ____________ and other animals.
c. Animals might ____________ to warmer places during cold weather.

6 Complete the outline.

Animals' Needs

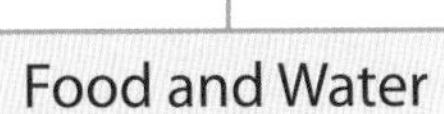

Food and Water	Oxygen	Shelter
• Give animals energy • Need more food and water as they [a] ________ bigger	• Is air to [b] ________ • Land animals breathe with lungs. • Fish breathe with [c] ________.	• Is a place to live • Protects animals from the weather and other [d] ________

Vocabulary Builder

Write the correct word and the meaning in Chinese.

1

to continue to live

____

2

a place to live

____

3

to move to another part of the world for warmer weather at a particular time of the year

____

4

to sleep all the time during the winter

____

Vocabulary Review 4

A **Complete the sentences with the words below.**

seeds	carbon dioxide	chloroplasts	flowers
cones	broad leaves	chlorophyll	process

1 A plant's __________ are what let it reproduce.

2 Flowering plants have flowers and produce seeds in __________.

3 Conifers do not have flowers. Instead, they produce their seeds in __________.

4 Deciduous trees have __________ __________ that usually change color in the fall.

5 Plants make their own food in a __________ called photosynthesis.

6 First, when the sun shines on a leaf, the __________ absorbs sunlight.

7 Then, the __________ use carbon dioxide, water, and the sun's energy to make sugar.

8 As photosynthesis occurs, the plant takes in __________ __________ from the air.

B **Complete the sentences with the words below.**

without	keeps	backbones	vertebrates
divided	needs	respond	fuel

1 One way to classify animals is by whether or not they have __________.

2 All mammals, birds, reptiles, fish, and amphibians are __________.

3 An animal __________ a backbone is called an invertebrate.

4 All vertebrates can be further __________ into two classes: warm-blooded animals and cold-blooded animals.

5 All animals have basic __________ to live and grow.

6 Like __________ runs a machine, all animals need energy to work.

7 A shelter __________ animals safe from the weather and from other animals.

8 Animals also __________ to changes in their environment to survive.

C Write the correct word and the meaning in Chinese.

1 plants that have flowers and produce seeds in flowers

____

2 trees that have needles and stay green all year long

____

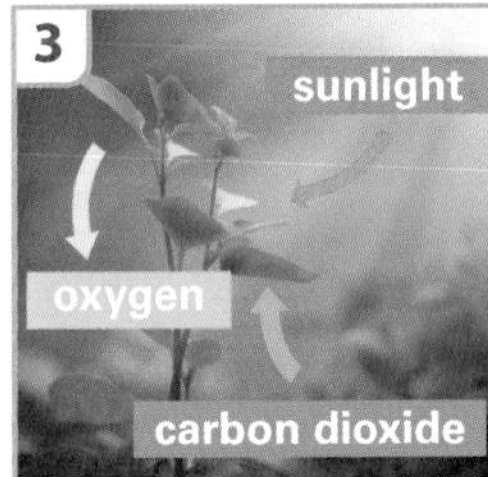

3 the process plants use to make food

____

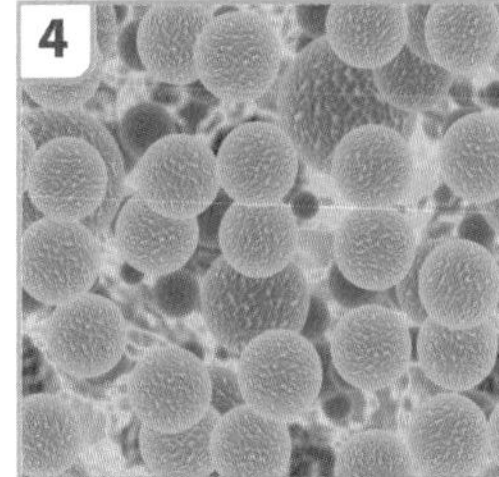

4 the green substance in a leaf

____

5 an animal without a backbone

____

6 to move to another part of the world for warmer weather at a particular time of the year

____

D Match each word with the correct definition and write the meaning in Chinese.

1 deciduous trees ____________ ☐

2 reproduce ____________ ☐

3 take in ____________ ☐

4 give off ____________ ☐

5 trait ____________ ☐

6 invertebrate ____________ ☐

7 regulate ____________ ☐

8 stay alive ____________ ☐

9 migrate ____________ ☐

10 hibernate ____________ ☐

a. to control
b. to absorb
c. to release
d. to survive
e. an animal without a backbone
f. a particular characteristic or quality
g. to sleep all the time during the winter
h. trees that have broad leaves that drop in winter
i. to make new living things; to generate offspring
j. to move to another part of the world for warmer weather at a particular time of the year

Unit 17

Food Chains

What Makes up a Food Chain?

Key Words

- organism
- connect
- food chain
- dependent upon
- decompose
- provide
- nutrient
- producer
- consumer
- decomposer
- break down
- make up

Animals cannot make their own food. They get their food by eating other organisms. Some animals eat plants. Others eat animals. And most animals are connected with one another on the food chain.

The food chain shows how all organisms are dependent upon one another for food.

For instance, at the bottom of the food chain, a plant uses the sun to make its own food. Then, a rabbit may eat the plant. Next, a fox may eat the rabbit. Later, a wolf may eat the fox. Finally, the wolf dies, and its body decomposes. This provides nutrients for the ground so that more plants may grow.

All organisms on the planet are producers, consumers, or decomposers. Producers, like plants, make their own food. Consumers are organisms that eat producers or other consumers. Animals are consumers. And decomposers are organisms that break down, or decompose, other organisms. Together, they all make up the food chain.

Organisms are connected with one another on the food chain.

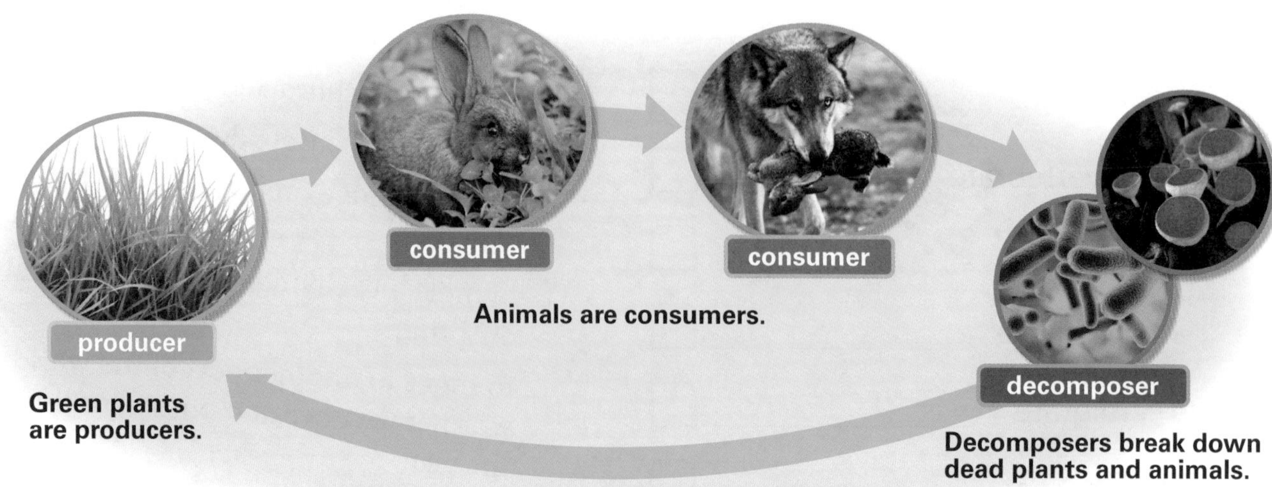

Main Idea and Details

1 **What is the passage mainly about?**

a. Producers and consumers.
b. Decomposers.
c. The food chain.

2 **A ______________ breaks down other organisms.**

a. consumer b. producer c. decomposer

3 **What animal on the food chain may eat a fox?**

a. A wolf. b. A rabbit. c. A plant.

4 **What does connected with mean?**

a. Friends with. b. Depended on. c. Linked with.

5 **According to the passage, which statement is true?**

a. All animals eat plants.
b. A producer makes its own food.
c. A decomposer makes food for other animals.

6 **Complete the outline.**

The Food Chain

- Shows how organisms [a] __________ on other organisms for food
- Plant → rabbit → fox → wolf → body decomposes → nutrients go into the ground to help [b] __________

- Producers = organisms that make food
- Consumers = organisms that eat producers or other [c] __________
- Decomposers = organisms that [d] __________ down other organisms

Vocabulary Builder

Write the correct word and the meaning in Chinese.

1 
a series of living things in which each uses the next lower member as a source of food

____

2 
an organism that makes food like green plants

____

3 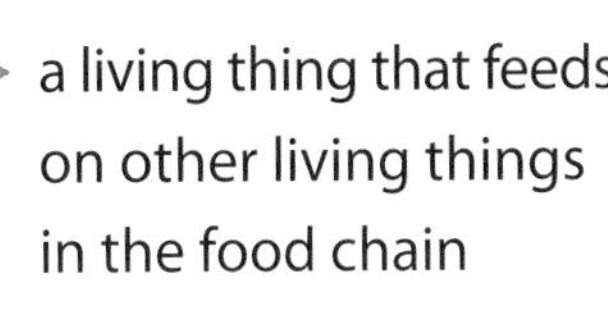
a living thing that feeds on other living things in the food chain

____

4 
to decay; to break down

____

Unit 18

Food Chains

Herbivores, Carnivores, and Omnivores

Key Words

- herbivore
- carnivore
- omnivore
- plant eater
- prey animal
- meat eater
- hunt
- predator
- vegetation
- overlap
- path
- food web

All animals need to eat to survive. Different consumers eat different kinds of food. There are three types of animals according to the food they eat. They are herbivores, carnivores, and omnivores.

Herbivores are animals that only eat plants. We call these animals plant eaters. There are many kinds of herbivores. They can be small, like rabbits, or they can be big, like cows. Elephants are herbivores as well. These animals are also often called prey animals.

Carnivores are meat eaters. They often hunt prey animals and kill other animals. Lions, tigers, and sharks are dangerous carnivores. Carnivores are often called predators.

Some animals eat both meat and vegetation. We call these animals omnivores. Wolves and pigs are omnivores. Humans are omnivores as well.

Food chains can overlap. They do not follow a single path. Several food chains that overlap form a food web. A food web shows how food chains are connected.

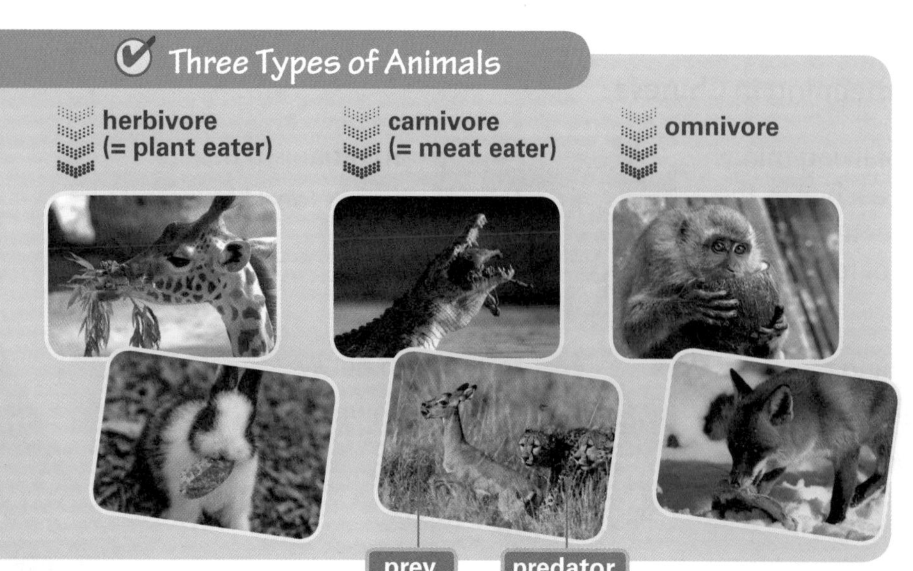

Main Idea and Details

1 **What is the main idea of the passage?**

a. Carnivores are meat eaters.

b. Animals eat different kinds of food.

c. Wolves, pigs, and humans are omnivores.

2 **A shark is ________.**

a. a carnivore b. an omnivore c. a herbivore

3 **What is another name for many herbivores?**

a. Prey animals. b. Predators. c. Meat eaters.

4 **What does types mean?**

a. Traits. b. Characteristics. c. Kinds.

5 **Answer the questions.**

a. Which animals are plant eaters? ________________

b. What do carnivores eat? ________________

c. What do omnivores eat? ________________

6 **Complete the outline.**

Types of Animals

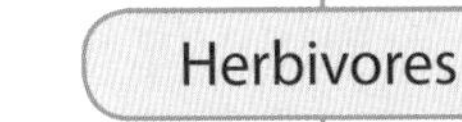

- **Herbivores**
  - Are [a] ________ eaters
  - Include rabbits, cows, and [b] ________
  - Are often called prey animals
- **Carnivores**
  - Are [c] ________ eaters
  - Hunt and kill prey animals
  - Include lions, tigers, and sharks
  - Are called [d] ________
- **Omnivores**
  - Eat both meat and vegetation
  - Include wolves, pigs, and [e] ________

Vocabulary Builder

Write the correct word and the meaning in Chinese.

1 

an animal that only eats plants; a plant eater ________________

2 

an animal that eats other animals; a meat eater ________________

3 

an animal that eats both plants and other animals ________________

4 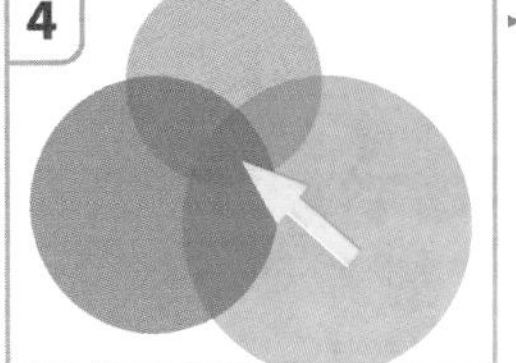

to cover part of the edge of something ________________

Unit 19

Ecosystems

What Are Ecosystems?

Key Words

- environment
- living thing
- nonliving thing
- surround
- depend on
- ecosystem
- desert
- grassland
- be made up of
- be filled with
- compete
- collect
- adapt

We live in an environment. An environment is all the living and nonliving things that surround us.

Plants and animals depend on one another in an environment. They depend on nonliving things, too, like water, air, and soil. Together, all the living and nonliving things in an area form an ecosystem.

The earth has many different ecosystems. There are desert, forest, grassland, lake, and ocean ecosystems.

Different kinds of ecosystems are made up of different kinds of plants and animals. Many trees and animals can be found in a forest. A lake is filled with fish, frogs, and insects.

The organisms in these ecosystems compete against each other to survive. Desert plants compete for water. Predators compete for prey. Prey animals such as rabbits and squirrels compete to collect food.

Ecosystems are constantly changing. So the plants and animals must adapt to these changes, too. Organisms that adapt will survive. Organisms that do not adapt will not survive.

Different Kinds of Ecosystems

Main Idea and Details

1 **What is the main idea of the passage?**

a. There are desert, ocean, and forest ecosystems.

b. Animals must change to survive.

c. The earth has many different ecosystems.

2 **Fish, frogs, and insects might live in a ________ ecosystem.**

a. desert **b.** lake **c.** forest

3 **What do desert plants compete for?**

a. Food. **b.** Water. **c.** Sunlight.

4 **What does collect mean?**

a. Hunt. **b.** Consume. **c.** Gather.

5 **Answer the questions.**

a. What is an environment? ________

b. What kinds of ecosystems are there? ________

c. What must organisms do when an ecosystem changes? ________

6 **Complete the outline.**

The Earth

Environments

- Are all the living and [a] ________ things in an area
- Plants and animals [b] ________ on one another.
- Also depend on nonliving things like water, air, and soil

Ecosystems

- There are desert, forest, grassland, lake, and [c] ________ ecosystems.
- Different animals and plants live in different ecosystems.
- Compete against each other
- Must [d] ________ to survive

Vocabulary Builder

Write the correct word and the meaning in Chinese.

1 

all the living and nonliving things in an area ________

2 

something that is not living or that is inanimate ________

3 

to try to win or gain something ________

4 

to get things and keep them together for a particular reason ________

Unit 20

Ecosystems

Dinosaurs: Extinct but Still Popular

Key Words

- be affected
- dinosaur
- vicious
- fierce
- pack
- in packs
- fearsome
- die out
- asteroid
- planet
- become extinct
- respond to
- endangered
- perish

Ecosystems can change. When a large change occurs, the organisms that live in that ecosystem are affected. Some even have trouble surviving.

Do you like dinosaurs? They lived on Earth millions of years ago. Some dinosaurs, like brontosaurus and triceratops, were huge. They were herbivores. But there were many vicious predators, too. Velociraptors were fierce predators that hunted in packs. And Tyrannosaurus rex was the most fearsome dinosaur of all.

However, around 65 million years ago, the dinosaurs suddenly died out. Scientists think that a large asteroid hit the earth then. It completely changed the planet. The weather on the earth got colder, and the sun shone less. The planet's ecosystems all changed. Many plants and animals died. The dinosaurs could not adapt, so they became extinct, too. No dinosaurs live on Earth now.

Many organisms are becoming extinct even today. If they are not able to respond to changes in their environment, some endangered animals may perish.

✓ Dinosaurs lived on Earth 65 million years ago.

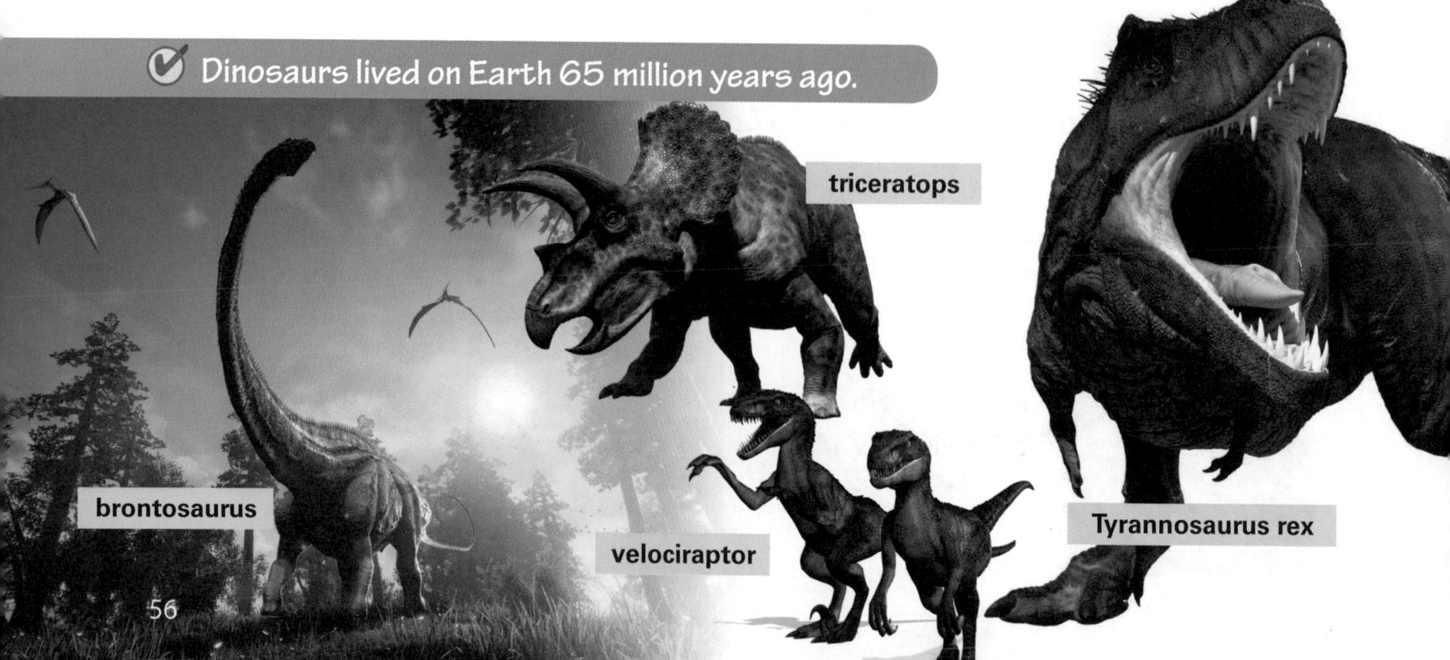

Main Idea and Details

1 **What is the passage mainly about?**

a. Why people like dinosaurs.
b. Why some animals are extinct.
c. Why an asteroid hit the earth.

2 **A large asteroid hit the earth ______________.**

a. 65 years ago b. 6,500 years ago c. 65,000,000 years ago

3 **Which dinosaurs hunted in packs?**

a. Velociraptor. b. Brontosaurus. c. Tyrannosaurus rex.

4 **What does perish mean?**

a. Die out. b. Reproduce. c. Adapt.

5 **According to the passage, which statement is true?**

a. Triceratops was a fearsome predator.
b. There are no dinosaurs on the earth today.
c. An asteroid hit the earth and made it warmer.

6 **Complete the outline.**

Dinosaurs

Lives

- There were [a] ______________ like brontosaurus and triceratops.
- There were [b] ______________ like velociraptor and Tyrannosaurus rex.
- Lived millions of years ago

Becoming Extinct

- Asteroid hit the earth 65 [c] ______________ years ago.
- Earth became colder.
- Dinosaurs could not adapt.
- Dinosaurs died out.
- There are no [d] ______________ on the earth today.

Vocabulary Builder

Write the correct word and the meaning in Chinese.

1 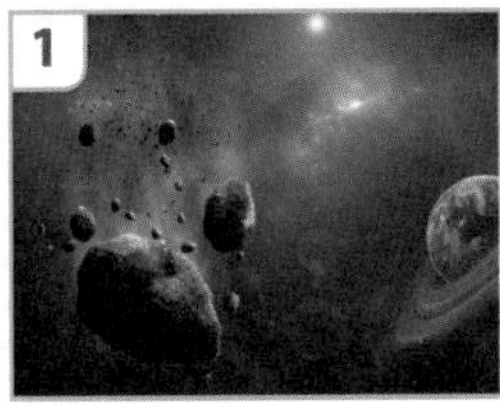
a mass of rock that moves around in space

____

2 
very violent and cruel; ready to attack

____

3 
a group of wild animals living and hunting together

____

4 
to disappear completely

____

Vocabulary Review 5

A **Complete the sentences with the words below.**

break down	prey animals	organisms	plants
according to	connected with	dependent	food chains

1 Most animals are ____________ ________ one another on the food chain.

2 The food chain shows how all organisms are ____________ upon one another for food.

3 All ____________ on the planet are producers, consumers, or decomposers.

4 Decomposers are organisms that ________ ________, or decompose, other organisms.

5 There are three types of animals ____________ ______ the food they eat.

6 Herbivores are animals that only eat ________.

7 Carnivores often hunt ________ __________ and kill other animals.

8 A food web shows how ________ _________ are connected.

B **Complete the sentences with the words below.**

brontosaurus	affected	in packs	form
made up of	compete	environment	extinct

1 An ______________ is all the living and nonliving things that surround us.

2 Together, all the living and nonliving things in an area ______ an ecosystem.

3 Different kinds of ecosystems are ________ ______ _____ different kinds of plants and animals.

4 The organisms in these ecosystems ___________ against each other to survive.

5 When a large change occurs, the organisms that live in that ecosystem are __________.

6 Some dinosaurs, like ______________ and triceratops, were herbivores.

7 Velociraptors were fierce predators that hunted ______ _________.

8 The dinosaurs could not adapt, so they became __________, too.

C Write the correct word and the meaning in Chinese.

1 

an individual living thing

____

2 

to change your behavior so that it is easier to live in a particular place

____

3 

an animal that eats other animals; a meat eater

____

4 

an animal that is hunted by other animals

____

5 

an organism like bacteria that breaks down other organisms

____

6 

a large reptile that lived 65 million years ago

____

D Match each word with the correct definition and write the meaning in Chinese.

1 organism ____________ ☐
2 ecosystem ____________ ☐
3 decompose ____________ ☐
4 depend on ____________ ☐
5 compete ____________ ☐
6 adapt ____________ ☐
7 predator ____________ ☐
8 vicious ____________ ☐
9 fearsome ____________ ☐
10 become extinct ____________ ☐

a. to adjust
b. to die out
c. to rely on
d. a living thing
e. to decay; to break down
f. to try to win or gain something
g. very frightening; causing fear
h. an animal that hunts others for food
i. very violent and cruel; ready to attack
j. all the living and nonliving things in an area

The Weather

Key Words

- condition
- atmosphere
- temperature
- air pressure
- wind
- measure
- degree
- measurement
- Fahrenheit
- Celsius
- blow
- meteorologist
- instrument
- thermometer
- barometer
- anemometer

The weather is the condition of the atmosphere. The weather has three main characteristics: the temperature, the air pressure, and the wind.

The temperature tells us how hot or how cold it is. We measure the temperature in degrees. There are two measurement systems. They are Fahrenheit and Celsius. 32° Fahrenheit is the same as 0° Celsius.

The air pressure is the amount of force that is in the air. When there is low air pressure, it may rain or snow. When there is high air pressure, the weather is usually nice.

Wind occurs when the air moves. Sometimes, the wind can blow very hard. Other times, it might not blow at all.

The weather is constantly changing. Meteorologists use many instruments to measure the weather. Three important ones are thermometers, barometers, and anemometers. A thermometer measures the air temperature. A barometer measures the air pressure. And an anemometer measures the speed of the wind.

Three Main Characteristics of the Weather

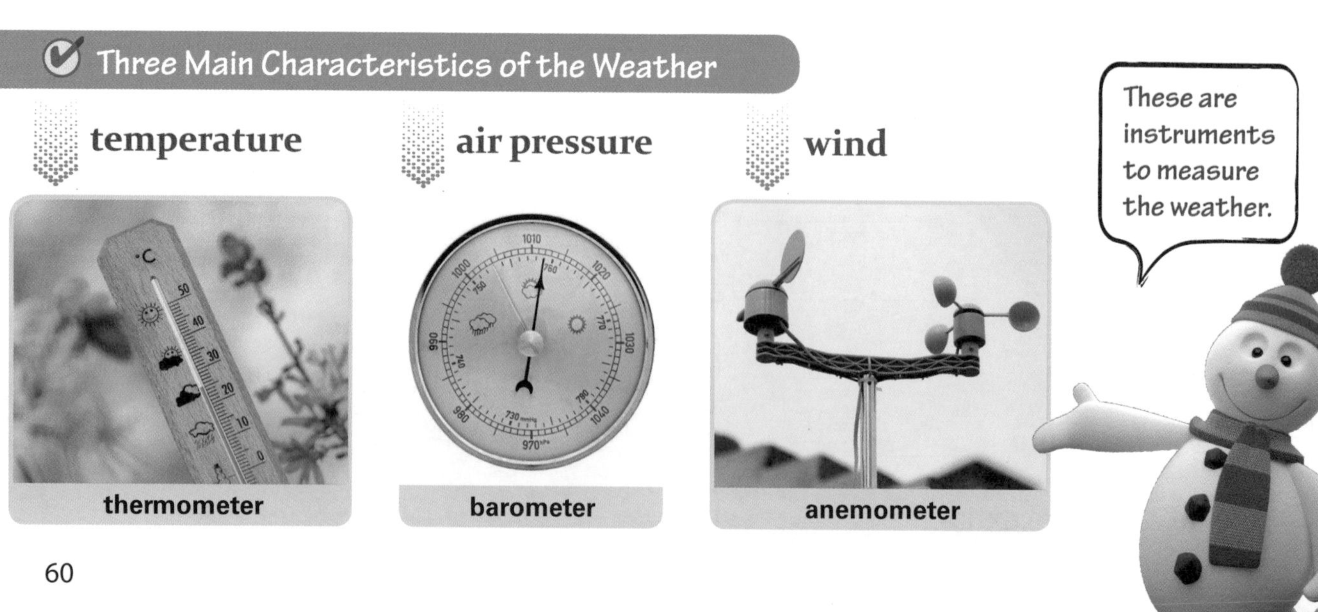

thermometer | barometer | anemometer

Main Idea and Details

1 What is the passage mainly about?

a. Thermometers, barometers, and anemometers.
b. How to measure the temperature.
c. The main characteristics of weather.

2 ______________ measures the air pressure.

a. An anemometer **b.** A thermometer **c.** A barometer

3 What is Celsius?

a. A temperature measuring system. **b.** A way to measure the air pressure.
c. A measurement of wind speed.

4 What does atmosphere mean?

a. Air. **b.** Air pressure. **c.** Weather.

5 Answer the questions.

a. What are two temperature measurement systems? ______________________
b. What happens when the air pressure is low? ______________________
c. What does a barometer measure? ______________________

6 Complete the outline.

Weather

- **Temperature**
  - How hot or cold it is
  - Is measured in Fahrenheit and [a] __________
  - [b] ______________ = measures the temperature
- **Air Pressure**
  - The amount of force in the air
  - Low air pressure = rain or snow
  - High [c] _____ __________ = nice weather
  - Barometer = [d] __________ the air pressure
- **Wind**
  - Happens when the air moves
  - Can blow hard or not at all
  - Anemometer = measures the [e] ________ ________

Vocabulary Builder

Write the correct word and the meaning in Chinese.

1

the amount of force in the air

____

2

the whole mass of air that surrounds the earth

____

3

equipment that measures the wind speed

____

4

a system for measuring temperature in which water freezes at 32° and boils at 212°

____

The Water Cycle

Key Words

- constant
- water cycle
- evaporation
- condensation
- precipitation
- liquid
- evaporate
- water vapor
- gaseous
- condense
- water droplet
- release
- flow into
- body of water

There is a constant amount of water on the earth. However, this water often changes forms. We call these changes the water cycle.

There are three stages in the water cycle: evaporation, condensation, and precipitation.

There is water in rivers, lakes, and oceans. The water is liquid. The sun often shines on this water. The sun's heat causes some of the water to evaporate. So it turns into water vapor, a gaseous form of water.

This water vapor rises into the atmosphere. As it gets higher in the air, the temperature decreases. So the water vapor condenses and becomes liquid again. These water droplets form into clouds. Actually, clouds are made of billions of water droplets. Sometimes, the clouds become too heavy, so they release their water. It falls to the ground as rain, snow, or ice.

Some water gets absorbed into the ground. But, other times, it flows into bodies of water. Then, the water cycle starts all over again.

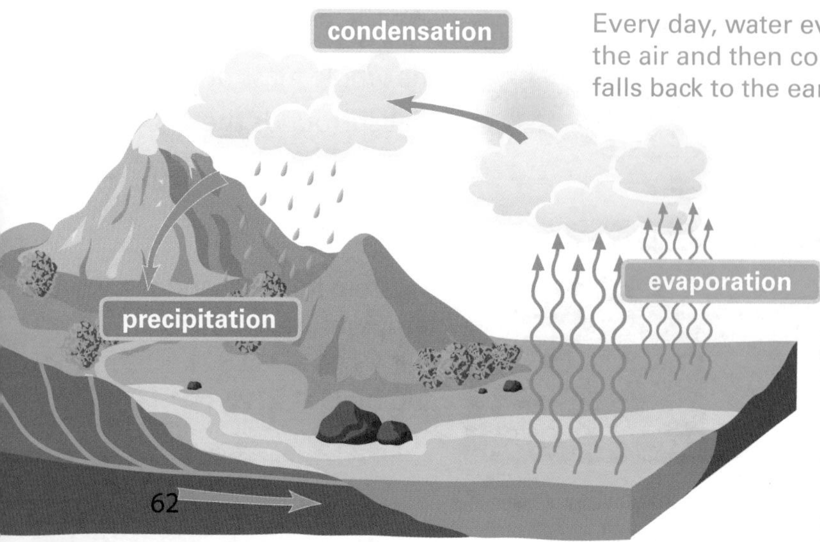

Every day, water evaporates into the air and then condenses and falls back to the earth.

water droplet

water vapor

Main Idea and Details

1 **What is the main idea of the passage?**

a. The water cycle has three stages. b. Precipitation can be rain, snow, or ice.
c. There is very much water on the earth.

2 **The sun's heat can make water ______________.**

a. flow b. evaporate c. condense

3 **What happens when water evaporates?**

a. It becomes water vapor. b. It falls as precipitation.
c. It becomes water droplets.

4 **What does decreases mean?**

a. Goes away. b. Goes up. c. Goes down.

5 **Answer the questions.**

a. What are the three stages in the water cycle? ______________________
b. What are clouds made of? ______________________
c. What are some forms of precipitation? ______________________

6 **Complete the outline.**

The Water Cycle

Evaporation	Condensation	Precipitation
• Sun's [a] ________ makes water warm. • Evaporates and turns into water vapor • Water vapor = [b] ________ form of water	• Water vapor rises. • Temperature decreases. • Water vapor condenses → becomes [c] ________ ________ • Forms clouds	• Clouds become heavy → [d] ________ water • Precipitation = rain, snow, and ice • Water gets absorbed into ground. • Water [e] ________ ________ other bodies of water.

Vocabulary Builder

Write the correct word and the meaning in Chinese.

1

the cycle of processes by which water circulates between the earth's oceans, atmosphere, and land

____

2

to change into water vapor

____

3
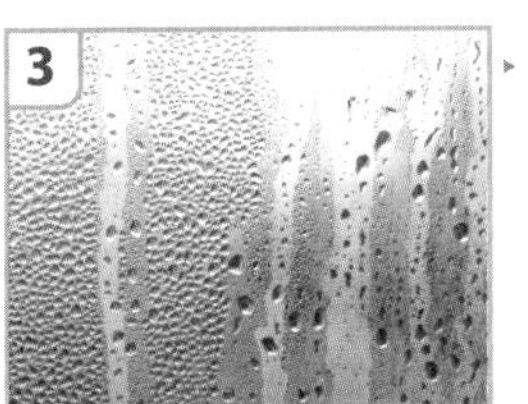
to become a liquid as it becomes cooler

____

4

a large area of water

____

Unit 23

Earth's Resources

Rocks, Minerals, and Soil

Key Words

- rock
- mineral
- soil
- igneous rock
- sedimentary rock
- metamorphic rock
- form
- harden
- substance
- element
- crystal

The earth's crust is made up of rocks, minerals, and soil. There are three major types of rocks. They are igneous, sedimentary, and metamorphic rocks.

Igneous rocks are very hard. They form when melted rock cools and hardens. Granite and basalt are igneous rocks.

Sedimentary rocks are much softer. They form when layers of sand, mud, and pebbles are pressed together. Limestone and sandstone are sedimentary rocks.

Metamorphic rocks are rocks that have changed from one type of rock into another. Marble and quartz are common metamorphic rocks.

Rocks are made of many kinds of minerals. A mineral is a solid substance found in nature. Minerals can be elements like carbon, iron, or gold. Or they can be crystals like quartz.

Soil is made of many different materials. These include small bits of rocks and minerals. Silt, clay, sand, and humus are all soil. We use soil to grow plants in.

Main Idea and Details

1 What is the passage mainly about?

a. Marble, limestone, and quartz.
b. Different kinds of rocks and soil.
c. Various minerals.

2 ____________ is a kind of sedimentary rock.

a. Basalt b. Marble c. Sandstone

3 How do igneous rocks form?

a. Melted rock cools and hardens.
b. Minerals combine to form rocks.
c. Rocks change from one form to another.

4 What does common mean?

a. Rare. b. Valuable. c. Usual.

5 According to the passage, which statement is true?

a. Granite is an igneous rock.
b. Basalt is a sedimentary rock.
c. Limestone is a metamorphic rock.

6 Complete the outline.

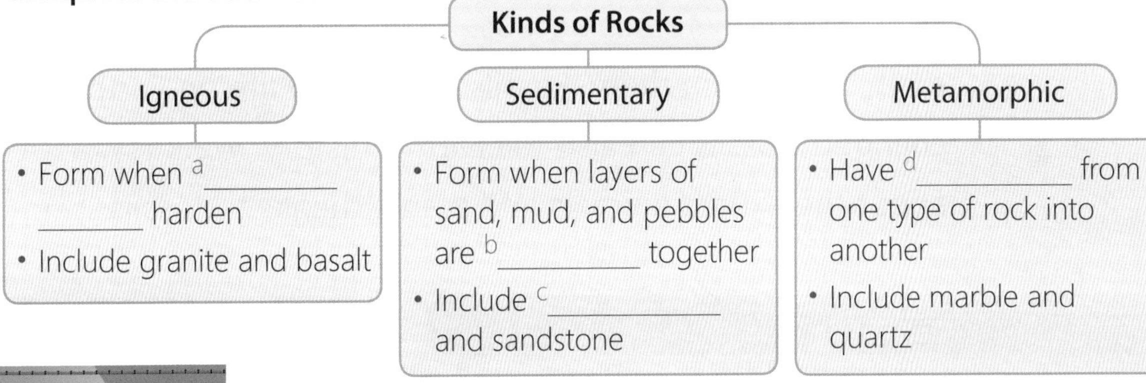

Vocabulary Builder

Write the correct word and the meaning in Chinese.

1 a kind of rock that has changed from another type of rock ____________

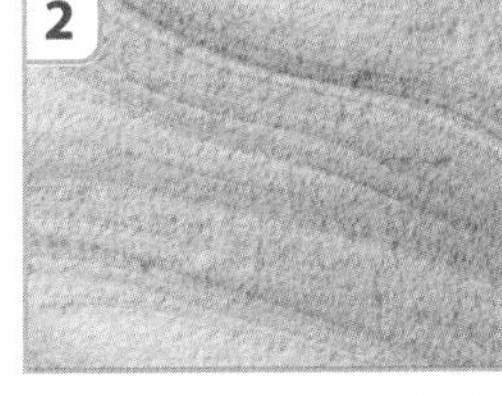

2 rock formed from sediments ____________

3 a solid substance that is formed naturally in rocks ____________

4 a substance such as carbon or iron ____________

Unit 24

Earth's Resources

Fossils and Fossil Fuels

Key Words

- woolly mammoth
- fossil
- remains
- footprint
- impression
- amber
- coal
- fossil fuel
- extinct
- thanks to

Woolly mammoths lived thousands of years ago. But they are not alive on Earth now. The dinosaurs are also not alive. Then, how do we know about them? We learn about them from their fossils.

What are fossils? Fossils are the remains of dead plants or animals that lived long ago. It takes them a very long time to form. Shells, teeth, and bones can become fossils. A fossil can even be a footprint or impression in rock. Most fossils are found in sedimentary rocks. Fossils are also found in amber.

We get fuel from fossils, too. Coal, oil, and natural gas are fossil fuels. Fossil fuels formed from the remains of plants and animals that died long ago.

Scientists study fossils because they can learn much about the earth's past from them. Fossils tell us how life on Earth has changed. Fossils can also tell Earth's history. We know a lot about the extinct animals and plants thanks to fossils.

Main Idea and Details

1 **What is the main idea of the passage?**

a. Scientists often study fossils.
b. Coal, oil, and natural gas are fossil fuels.
c. Fossils and fossil fuels come from the past.

2 **There are some fossils in ____________.**

a. amber   b. oil   c. natural gas

3 **Where are most fossils found?**

a. In coal.   b. In sedimentary rock.   c. In amber.

4 **What does found mean?**

a. Manufactured.   b. Reported.   c. Discovered.

5 **Complete the sentences.**

a. Fossils can be shells, ____________, or bones.
b. Fossil fuels formed from the remains of dead plants and ____________.
c. Scientists study ____________ to learn about the earth's past.

6 **Complete the outline.**

Dead Organisms

Fossils
- Are the remains of dead plants and animals
- Can be shells, teeth, or [a] ________
- Form in sedimentary rocks and [b] ________
- Can tell scientists much about the past

Fossil Fuels
- Are coal, oil, and [c] ________ ________
- Form from the [d] ________ of plants and animals that died long ago

Vocabulary Builder

Write the correct word and the meaning in Chinese.

1 
the parts of something that are left after the rest has been destroyed
____

2 
a fuel formed in the earth from plant or animal remains
____

3 
a hard yellow-brown substance used for making jewelry
____

4 
a mark left by pressing something into a surface
____

2 Science

Review 6

A **Complete the sentences with the words below.**

Fahrenheit	constant	water droplets	force
atmosphere	instruments	evaporation	condenses

1 The weather is the condition of the ______________.

2 We measure the temperature in degrees. 32° ______________ is the same as 0° Celsius.

3 The air pressure is the amount of __________ that is in the air.

4 Meteorologists use many ______________ to measure the weather.

5 There is a ____________ amount of water on the earth.

6 There are three stages in the water cycle: ______________, condensation, and precipitation.

7 As the water vapor gets higher in the air, it ______________ and becomes liquid again.

8 Actually, clouds are made of billions of __________ ____________.

B **Complete the sentences with the words below.**

woolly mammoths	sedimentary	minerals	fossils
melted rock	remains	scientists	changed

1 The earth's crust is made up of rocks, ____________, and soil.

2 Igneous rocks form when __________ ________ cools and hardens.

3 ______________ rocks form when layers of sand, mud, and pebbles are pressed together.

4 Metamorphic rocks are rocks that have ____________ from one type of rock into another.

5 __________ ______________ lived thousands of years ago.

6 Fossils are the ___________ of dead plants or animals that lived long ago.

7 We get fuel from __________, too. Coal, oil, and natural gas are fossil fuels.

8 ____________ study fossils because they can learn much about the earth's past from them.

C Write the correct word and the meaning in Chinese.

1

a gaseous form of water; steam

____

2

water that falls to the ground as rain, snow, etc.

____

3

rock formed when melted rock cools and hardens

____

4

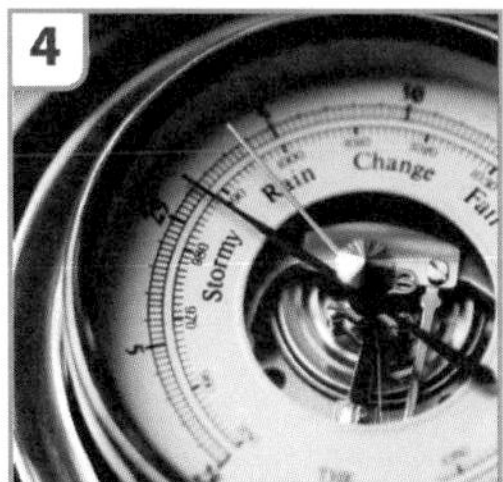

equipment that measures the air pressure

____

5

the remains of a dead plant or animal that lived long ago

____

6

a brown or black material in soil that is formed when plants and animals decay

____

D Match each word with the correct definition and write the meaning in Chinese.

1 evaporate ______________ ☐

2 condense ______________ ☐

3 air pressure ______________ ☐

4 meteorologist ______________ ☐

5 metamorphic rock ______________ ☐

6 igneous rock ______________ ☐

7 mineral ______________ ☐

8 harden ______________ ☐

9 remains ______________ ☐

10 footprint ______________ ☐

a. to become firm or stiff
b. to change into water vapor
c. a mark made by a foot or shoe
d. the amount of force in the air
e. a person who studies the weather
f. a kind of rock made from melted rock
g. to become a liquid as it becomes cooler
h. a solid substance that is formed naturally in rocks
i. a kind of rock that has changed from another type of rock
j. the parts of something that are left after the rest has been destroyed

Wrap-Up Test 2

A **Write the correct word for each section.**

depend on	ecosystems	oxygen	omnivores	needles
vertebrates	food chain	soil	condensation	fossils

1 As photosynthesis occurs, the plant gives off __________ into the air.

2 All __________ can be further divided into two classes: warm-blooded animals and cold-blooded animals.

3 Some animals eat both meat and vegetation. We call these animals __________.

4 Most animals are connected with one another on the __________ __________.

5 Evergreen trees have __________ instead of leaves and stay green all year long.

6 Plants and animals __________ __________ one another in an environment.

7 The organisms in these __________ compete against each other to survive.

8 There are three stages in the water cycle: evaporation, __________, and precipitation.

9 The earth's crust is made up of rocks, minerals, and __________.

10 __________ are the remains of dead plants or animals that lived long ago.

B **Write the meanings of the words in Chinese.**

1 flowering plant __________
2 conifer __________
3 deciduous tree __________
4 evergreen tree __________
5 take in __________
6 give off __________
7 trait __________
8 regulate __________
9 migrate __________
10 hibernate __________
11 shelter __________
12 photosynthesis __________
13 chlorophyll __________
14 chloroplast __________
15 carbon dioxide __________
16 backbone __________
17 vertebrate __________
18 invertebrate __________
19 warm-blooded animal __________
20 cold-blooded animal __________
21 carnivore __________
22 predator __________
23 precipitation __________
24 impression __________
25 evaporate __________
26 condense __________
27 meteorologist __________
28 sedimentary rock __________
29 metamorphic rock __________
30 igneous rock __________

3

- Mathematics
- Language
- Visual Arts
- Music

Unit 25

Geometry

Points, Lines, and Line Segments

Key Words

- dot
- line
- point
- line segment
- endlessly
- endpoint
- horizontal line
- vertical line
- diagonal line
- angle
- intersect
- right angle
- perpendicular lines
- side by side
- parallel lines

Make a dot on a piece of paper. Then, make another dot. Now, connect the two dots. You have just drawn a line. And the two dots are called points. You can give the points names like this: A B We call them point A and point B. The line that goes through points A and B is called line AB. It is written like this, too: $\overleftrightarrow{AB}$.

A segment is a part of something. A line segment is a part of a line. C D A line can go on endlessly, but a line segment has two endpoints. We call the line segment by its endpoints like this: line segment CD or $\overline{CD}$.

Lines can go in many different directions. A horizontal line goes from left to right. A vertical line goes up and down. A diagonal line moves at an angle.

Sometimes, two lines meet each other. We can say that these lines intersect one another. When a horizontal line and a vertical line intersect, they might form a right angle. The two lines that form a right angle are called perpendicular lines. If two lines run side by side and never meet, they are parallel lines.

Lines

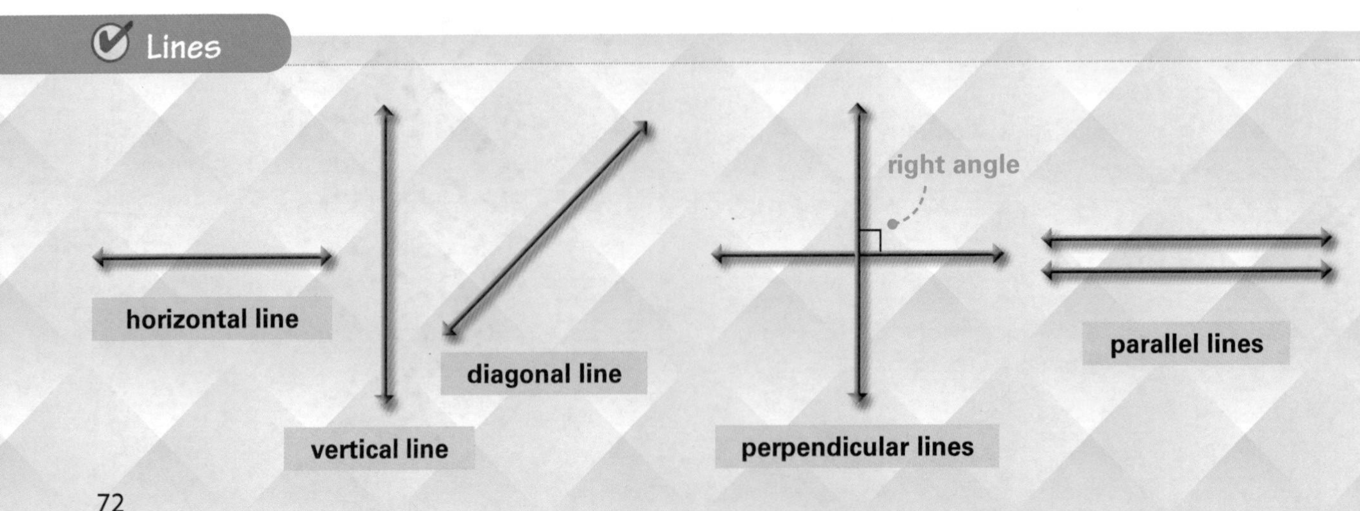

Main Idea and Details

1 **What is the main idea of the passage?**

a. There are many types of lines. **b.** Line segments are parts of lines.
c. We can mark points on lines.

2 **A dot on a line is called a ____________.**

a. segment **b.** point **c.** angle

3 **How does a vertical line move?**

a. Up and down. **b.** From left to right. **c.** At an angle.

4 **What does endlessly mean?**

a. Quickly. **b.** Again. **c.** Forever.

5 **Complete the sentences.**

a. A line that goes at an ____________ is a diagonal line.
b. Lines that are perpendicular ____________ a right angle.
c. ____________ lines run side by side and never meet.

6 **Complete the outline.**

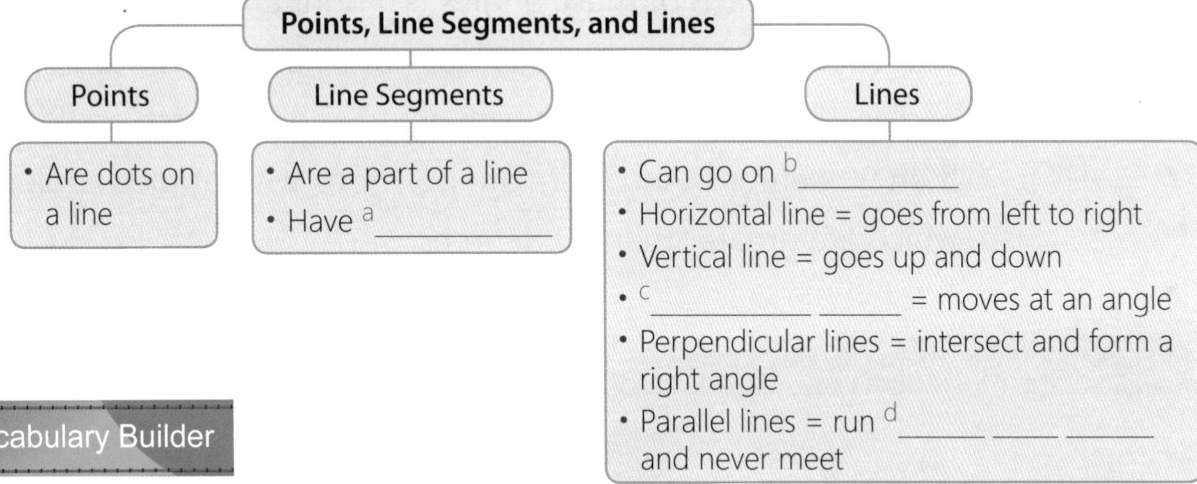

Vocabulary Builder

Write the correct word and the meaning in Chinese.

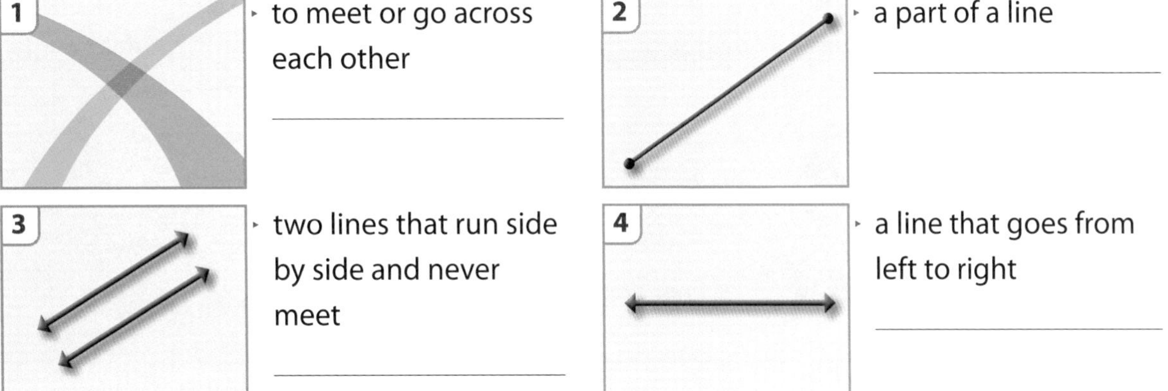

1 to meet or go across each other ____________

2 a part of a line ____________

3 two lines that run side by side and never meet ____________

4 a line that goes from left to right ____________

Unit 26

Geometry

Polygons

Key Words

- polygon
- closed figure
- triangle
- rectangle
- pentagon
- hexagon
- octagon
- right angle
- acute angle
- obtuse angle

There are many types of polygons. A polygon is made of three or more line segments. And it must be a closed figure. That means all of the lines in the polygon meet one another.

A polygon with three sides is a triangle. A polygon with four sides is a square or a rectangle. A five-sided polygon is a pentagon, a six-sided polygon is a hexagon, and an eight-sided polygon is an octagon.

When we create a polygon, the lines meet at certain points. When two lines meet, they create an angle.

For example, there are four sides to a square. So a square has four angles. Each of these angles is a right angle. This means that each angle is 90 degrees. But not all polygons have right angles. There are polygons with acute angles, which are less than 90 degrees. And there are polygons with obtuse angles, which are greater than 90 degrees.

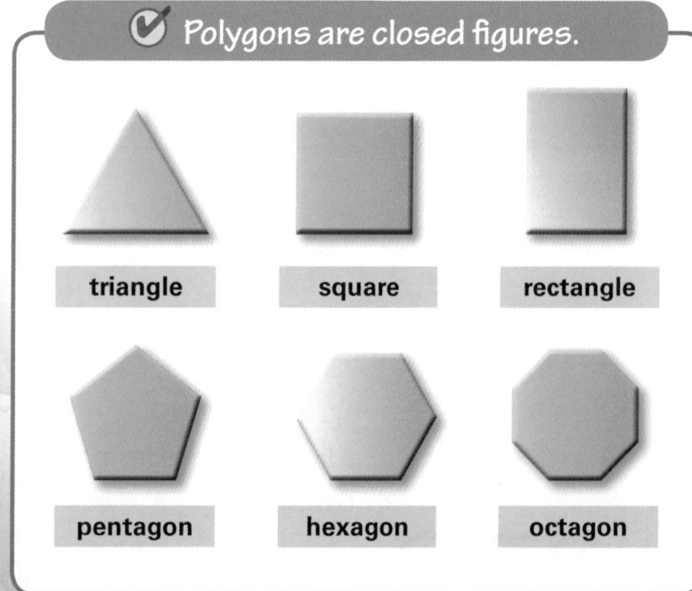

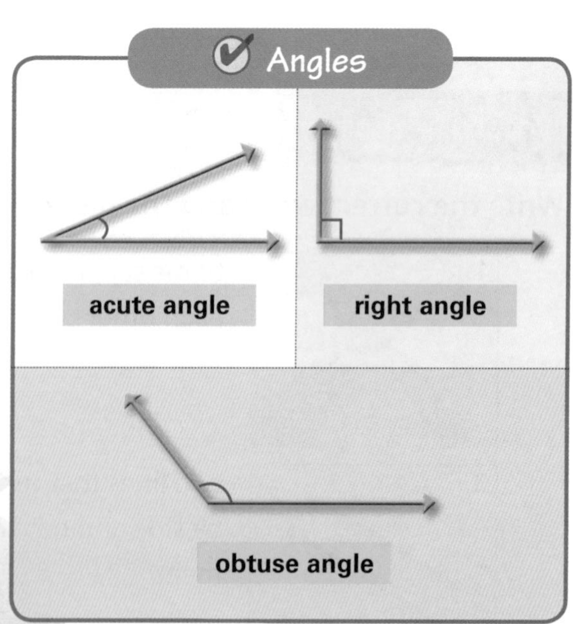

Main Idea and Details

1 **What is the passage mainly about?**

a. Polygons. b. Figures. c. Squares.

2 **A polygon with six sides is a ______________.**

a. triangle b. pentagon c. hexagon

3 **How many sides does an octagon have?**

a. 6 b. 7 c. 8

4 **What does less than mean?**

a. Under. b. Over. c. Equal to.

5 **According to the passage, which statement is true?**

a. A rectangle is a five-sided polygon.

b. A pentagon is a six-sided polygon.

c. A triangle is a three-sided polygon.

6 **Complete the outline.**

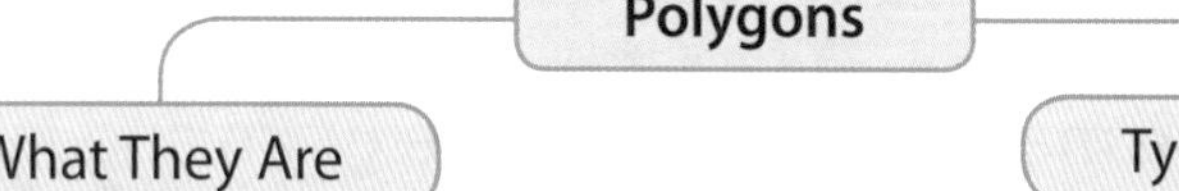

Polygons

What They Are

- Are [a] ________ figures
- Have three or more [b] ______ ____________
- All of the line segments meet one another.

Types of Polygons

- Triangle = 3 sides
- Square = 4 sides
- Rectangle = 4 sides
- Pentagon = 5 sides
- [c] ____________ = 6 sides
- Octagon = 8 sides
- Polygons might have right angles, acute angles, or [d] _________ _________.

Vocabulary Builder

Write the correct word and the meaning in Chinese.

1

a closed figure that has three or more line segments

____

2

an eight-sided polygon

____

3
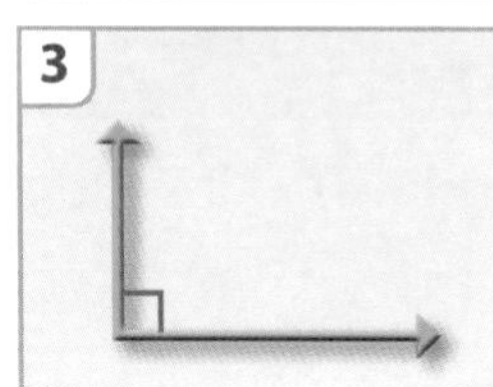

an angle that is 90 degrees

____

4
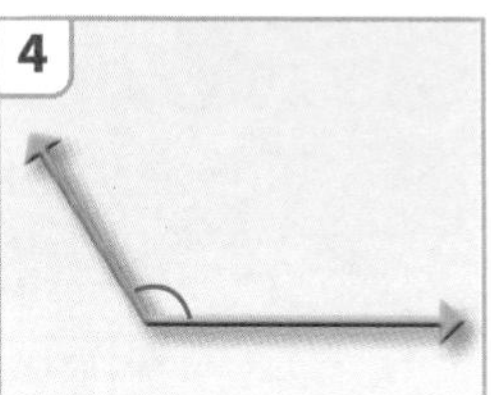

an angle that is greater than 90 degrees

____

Unit 27

Measurement

The U.S. Customary System and the Metric System

Key Words

- length
- weight
- capacity
- various
- measurement system
- U.S. customary system
- metric system
- be based on
- unit
- cup
- pint

We often need to know the length, weight, and capacity of various items. To measure them, we use measurement systems. There are two major systems: the U.S. customary system and the metric system.

The U.S. customary system is used in the United States. Most of the world uses the metric system. The metric system is based on units of ten. The U.S. customary system uses different types of measurements.

The metric system uses the meter to measure length. For smaller units, there are centimeters and millimeters. For bigger units, there are kilometers. The U.S. customary system uses the foot. There are 12 inches in one foot. For bigger units, it uses the mile.

For weight, the metric system uses the gram and kilogram. The U.S. customary system uses the ounce and the pound. There are 16 ounces in one pound.

And for capacity, the metric system uses the liter. The U.S. customary system uses the cup, pint, quart, and gallon.

Units of Length

Metric System		U.S. Customary System	
• millimeter (mm)		• inch (in)	1 in = 2.54 cm
• centimeter (cm)	1 cm = 10 mm	• foot (ft)	1 ft = 12 in
• meter (m)	1 m = 100 cm	• mile (mi)	1 mi = 5,280 ft
• kilometer (km)	1 km = 1,000 m		

Units of Weight and Capacity

Metric System		U.S. Customary System			
• gram (g)		• ounce (oz)		• pound (lb)	1 lb = 16 oz
• kilogram (kg)	1 kg = 1,000 g	• cup		• pint (pt)	1 pt = 2 cups
• liter (l)	1 l = 1,000 ml	• quart (qt)	1 qt = 2 pt	• gallon (gal)	1 gal = 4 qt

Main Idea and Details

1 **What is the passage mainly about?**

a. Kilograms and pounds.

b. Two measurement systems.

c. How to measure length.

2 **One unit of length is the ____________.**

a. pound b. inch c. liter

3 **What is an ounce?**

a. A unit of weight. b. A unit of length. c. A unit of capacity.

4 **What does various mean?**

a. Few. b. Several. c. Different.

5 **Answer the questions.**

a. Who uses the metric system? ____________________

b. How many inches are in a foot? ____________________

c. What is the unit of capacity in the metric system? ____________________

6 **Complete the outline.**

Measurement Systems

The U.S. Customary System
- Is used in the U.S.
- Length = a________, foot, and mile
- b__________ = ounce and pound
- Capacity = cup, pint, quart, and gallon

The Metric System
- Is used in most of the world
- Is based on units of ten
- Length = c________
- Weight = gram
- d__________ = liter

Vocabulary Builder

Write the correct word and the meaning in Chinese.

1 

a measurement system that Americans use ____________

2 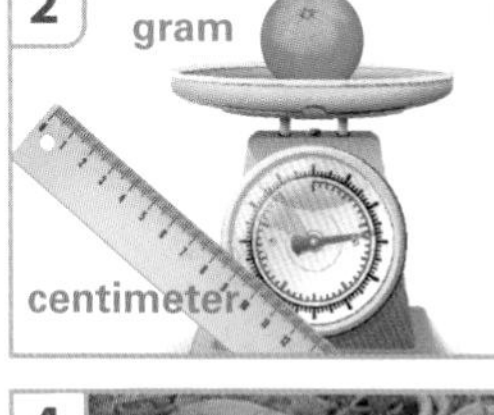

a measurement system that is based on units of ten ____________

3 
the amount a container can hold ____________

4 
a measurement of how heavy a person or thing is ____________

Unit 28

Measurement

Measurement Word Problems

Key Words

- word problem
- jog
- total
- string
- project
- ruler
- ham
- butcher
- thirsty
- convenience store
- soda

❶ John loves to jog. In the morning, he jogs 700 meters. In the afternoon, he jogs 1,200 meters. And in the evening, he jogs 800 meters. How many kilometers does he jog during the day?

⇨ He jogs a total of 2,700 meters. There are 1,000 meters in 1 kilometer.
2,700 ÷ 1,000 = 2.7. So he jogs 2.7 kilometers.

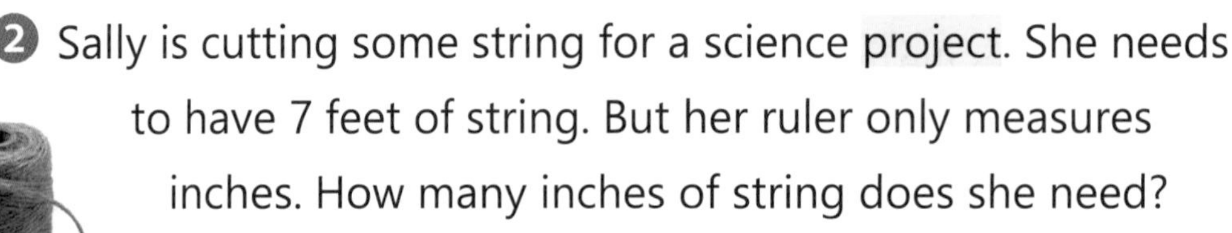

❷ Sally is cutting some string for a science project. She needs to have 7 feet of string. But her ruler only measures inches. How many inches of string does she need?

⇨ There are 12 inches in one foot. 7 × 12 = 84. So she needs 84 inches of string.

❸ James goes to the store to buy some ham. He asks the butcher to give him a pound and a half of ham. How many ounces of ham does he get?

⇨ There are 16 ounces in one pound.
1.5 × 16 = 24. He gets 24 ounces of ham.

❹ Diana is thirsty, so she goes to the convenience store for a drink. She buys a 500-milliliter can of soda. How many liters of soda does she buy?

⇨ There are 1,000 milliliters in one liter. 500 ÷ 1,000 = 0.5. She buys 0.5 liters of soda.

Main Idea and Details

1 **What is the passage mainly about?**

a. Changing from the metric system to the U.S. customary system.

b. Doing problems with word measurements.

c. The purchases that some people make.

2 **There are ________ meters in one kilometer.**

a. 100 b. 1,000 c. 10,000

3 **How many ounces are in a pound?**

a. 16 b. 32 c. 64

4 **What does project mean?**

a. Assignment.

b. Class.

c. Teacher.

5 **Complete the sentences.**

a. One ________ has 12 inches.

b. One pound has 16 ________.

c. One ________ has 1,000 milliliters.

Vocabulary Builder

Write the correct word and the meaning in Chinese.

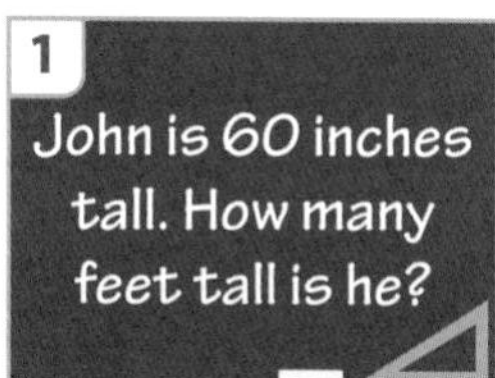

a mathematic question that is stated verbally

____

to run slowly as a form of exercise

____

the number or amount of everything counted

____

a shopkeeper who cuts up and sells meat

____

a store where you can buy food and other products and that is usually open 24 hours a day

____

feeling that you want or need to drink something

____

Vocabulary Review 7

A **Complete the sentences with the words below.**

parallel	line segment	intersect	polygon
points	perpendicular	octagon	obtuse

1 The line that goes through __________ A and B is called line AB.

2 A line can go on endlessly, but a ________ ____________ has two endpoints.

3 The two lines that form a right angle are called ________________ lines.

4 If two lines run side by side and never meet, they are ___________ lines.

5 When a horizontal line and a vertical line ____________, they might form a right angle.

6 A ____________ is made of three or more line segments.

7 A five-sided polygon is a pentagon, and an eight-sided polygon is an ____________.

8 There are polygons with __________ angles, which are greater than 90 degrees.

B **Complete the sentences with the words below.**

customary	based on	weight	measure
kilogram	milliliters	pound	capacity

1 We often need to know the length, __________, and capacity of various items.

2 The U.S. _____________ system is used in the United States.

3 The metric system is __________ _______ units of ten.

4 The metric system uses the meter to ____________ length.

5 For weight, the metric system uses the gram and ____________.

6 The U.S. customary system uses the ounce and the __________ for weight.

7 For ____________, the metric system uses the liter.

8 There are 1,000 ____________ in one liter.

C Write the correct word and the meaning in Chinese.

1

a five-sided polygon

____

2
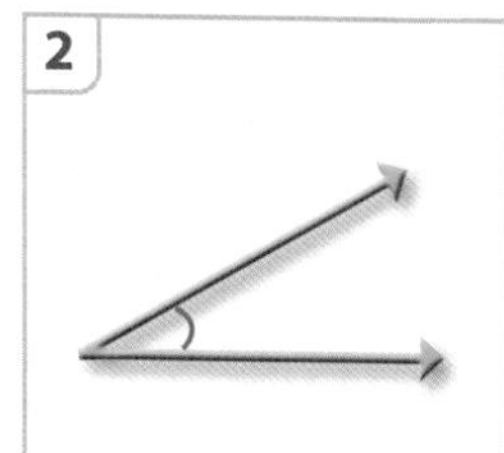
an angle that is less than 90 degrees

____

3

the number or amount of everything counted

____

4
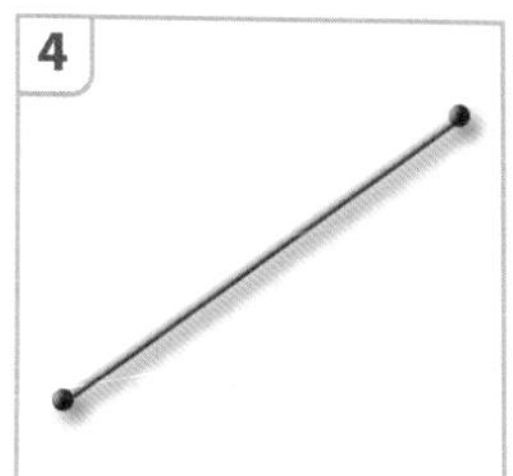
a part of a line

____

5
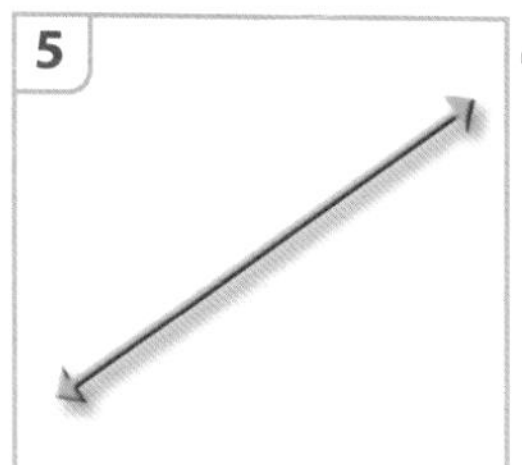
a line that moves at an angle

____

6
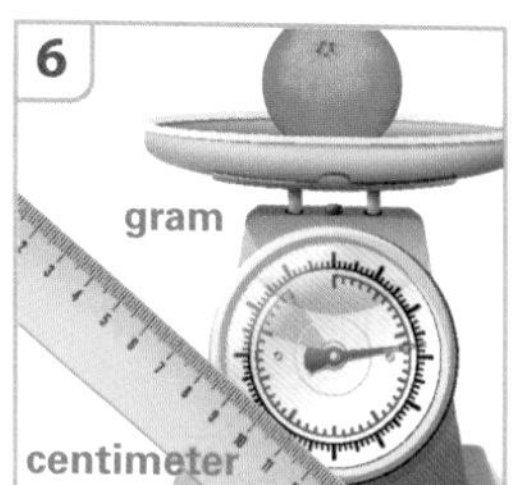

a measurement system that is based on units of ten

____

D Match each word with the correct definition and write the meaning in Chinese.

1 polygon ____________ ☐
2 acute angle ____________ ☐
3 perpendicular lines ____________ ☐
4 U.S. customary system ____________ ☐
5 capacity ____________ ☐
6 unit ____________ ☐
7 word problem ____________ ☐
8 jog ____________ ☐
9 project ____________ ☐
10 convenience store ____________ ☐

a. to run slowly as a form of exercise
b. the amount a container can hold
c. an angle that is less than 90 degrees
d. a measurement system that Americans use
e. a task that usually requires a lot of time and effort
f. a mathematic question that is stated verbally
g. the two lines that intersect and form a right angle
h. a closed figure that has three or more line segments
i. a single amount or quantity of something that is used as a standard measurement
j. a store where you can buy food and other products and that is usually open 24 hours a day

Unit 29

Myths From Ancient Greece

Gods and Goddesses in Greek Myths

Key Words

- ancient
- god
- goddess
- control
- myth
- normal
- magical power
- immortal
- the heavens
- the underworld
- marriage
- wisdom
- messenger
- twin

The ancient Greeks believed in many gods and goddesses. They believed the gods and goddesses lived on the highest mountain in Greece, called Mount Olympus. From there, they looked down on the earth and controlled people and nature.

In Greek myths, the gods and goddesses often acted like normal people. They ate, drank, and slept. They argued with each other, fell in love, and got married. However, they had magical powers and were immortal. They never died.

Zeus was the most powerful god. He was the king of the gods and ruled the heavens. His brother Poseidon was the god of the sea, and his other brother Hades was the god of the underworld.

Hera was Zeus's wife and the goddess of marriage. Athena was the goddess of wisdom, Ares was the god of war, and Aphrodite was the goddess of love and beauty. Hermes was the messenger of the gods. Apollo, a son of Zeus, was the god of light, and his twin sister Artemis was the goddess of the hunt.

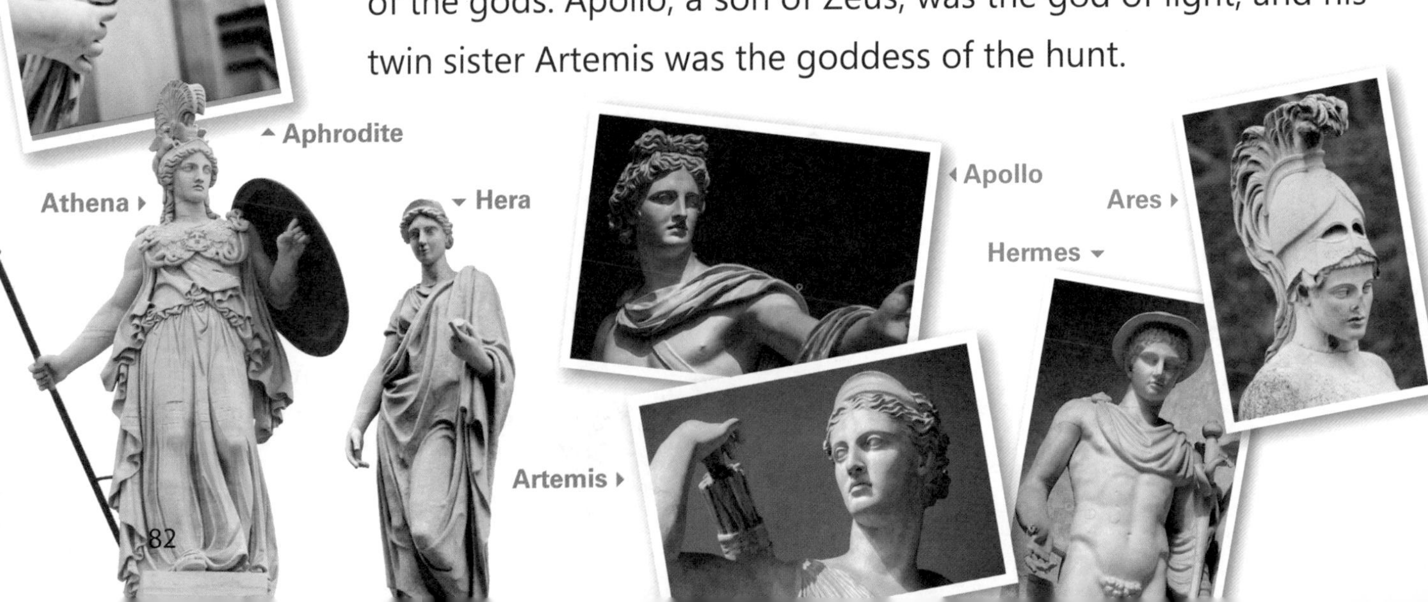

Main Idea and Details

1 **What is the main idea of the passage?**

a. Zeus, Poseidon, and Hades were three powerful gods.
b. The Greek gods all lived on Mount Olympus.
c. The ancient Greeks had many gods and goddesses.

2 **The messenger of the gods was ________.**

a. Hermes b. Athena c. Apollo

3 **Who was the goddess of love?**

a. Athena. b. Aphrodite. c. Hera.

4 **What does argued mean?**

a. Ate. b. Fought. c. Traveled.

5 **According to the passage, which statement is true?**

a. Zeus was the king of the gods. b. Athena was the goddess of the hunt.
c. Apollo was the god of the sea.

6 **Complete the outline.**

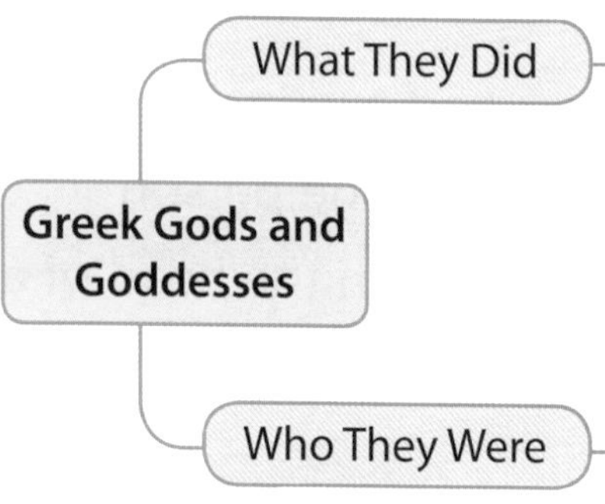

What They Did:
- Lived on a ________ ________
- Controlled people and nature
- Acted like normal people
- Had magical powers and were b ________

Who They Were:
- Zeus = king of the gods
- c ________ = god of the sea
- Hades = god of the underworld
- Hera = goddess of marriage
- d ________ = goddess of wisdom
- Ares = god of war
- Aphrodite = goddess of love
- Hermes = messenger of the gods
- e ________ = god of light
- Artemis = goddess of the hunt

Vocabulary Builder

Write the correct word and the meaning in Chinese.

1

the place where dead people go in Greek myths

____

2
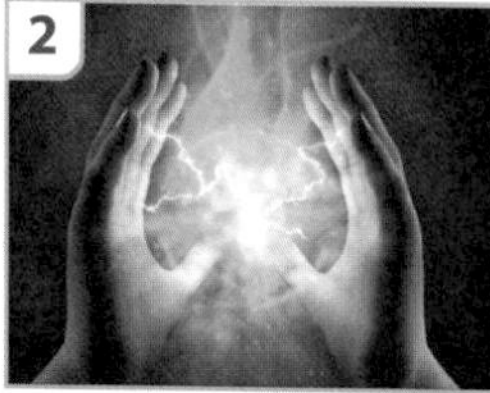
an ability to perform magic

____

3

living forever and never dying

____

4

being one of a pair born at one birth

____

Unit **30**

Myths From Ancient Greece

Titans, Heroes, and Monsters in Greek Myths

Key Words

- Titan
- hero
- monster
- giant
- punish
- demigod
- Medusa
- turn to
- Minotaur
- centaur
- satyr

Greek mythology had many Titans, heroes, and monsters as well as gods.

The Titans were powerful giants that fought, but lost to, the gods. Atlas was the strongest Titan. The gods punished him by making him hold the world up on his shoulders. Prometheus was a Titan who stole fire from the gods and took it to the people on Earth.

Greek myths had many heroes, too. These heroes were often demigods. So, one parent was human while the other was a god or goddess. The greatest hero of all was Heracles. He was a son of Zeus and the strongest man in the world. Perseus, Theseus, Achilles, and Odysseus were heroes, too.

Finally, there were many monsters. Medusa had a woman's head but snakes for hair. If anyone looked at Medusa, the person would turn to stone. The Minotaur was a man with the head of a bull. A centaur was part human and part horse. And satyrs were half man and half goat.

✔ Greek myths have many Titans and heroes.

Atlas

Prometheus

Heracles

Perseus

Theseus

Achilles

✔ Some mythical creatures are part human and part animal.

Medusa

Minotaur

centaur

satyr

Main Idea and Details

1 **What is the passage mainly about?**

a. Some of the most powerful Titans. b. Medusa and the Minotaur.

c. Characters from Greek mythology.

2 **A horse with the upper body of a man was a ____________.**

a. centaur b. Minotaur c. Medusa

3 **Who was the greatest Greek hero?**

a. Theseus. b. Heracles. c. Perseus.

4 **What does turn mean?**

a. Change. b. Order. c. Make.

5 **Answer the questions.**

a. What did Prometheus do? ______________________________

b. Who was the strongest Titan? ______________________________

c. What was a satyr? ______________________________

6 **Complete the outline.**

Greek Mythology

Titans	Heroes	Monsters
• Were powerful [a] ________ • Atlas = the strongest Titan; held the world up on his [b] ____________ • Prometheus = stole fire and gave it to man	• Were often demigods • [c] ____________ = the greatest hero • Perseus, Theseus, Achilles, and Odysseus	• Medusa = could turn people into [d] ________ • Minotaur = man with the head of a bull • Centaur = part human and part horse • [e] ________ = half man and half goat

Vocabulary Builder

Write the correct word and the meaning in Chinese.

1 

a powerful giant that fought the gods

____

2 

a child of a god or goddess and a human

____

3 

a monster that was part human and part horse

____

4 

a monster that was half man and half goat

____

3 Mathematics • Language • Visual Arts • Music

Unit 31

Myths From Ancient Rome

Same Gods, Different Names

Key Words

- spread
- Roman Empire
- worship
- mythology
- wisdom
- war
- love
- beauty

The ancient Greeks spread their culture to many other places. One of these places was the Roman Empire. The gods and goddesses of the ancient Greeks were also worshipped by the people of ancient Rome.

The Romans did not use the Greek names though. Instead, they gave their gods new names.

Zeus was the king of the gods in Greek mythology. But in Roman mythology, his name was Jupiter. Poseidon was the Greek god of the sea. But his Roman name was Neptune. And Hades was the Greek god of the underworld. But the Romans called him Pluto.

The other gods and goddesses got new names, too. Hera, the wife of Zeus, became Juno. Athena, the goddess of wisdom, became Minerva. Ares, the god of war, became Mars. Aphrodite, the goddess of love and beauty, became Venus. Artemis, the goddess of the hunt, was Diana. Hermes, the messenger of the gods, was Mercury. But, Apollo, the god of light, was called the same name: Apollo.

Different Names of Greek and Roman Gods and Goddesses

Greek Name	Roman Name	Greek Name	Roman Name
Zeus	Jupiter	Ares	Mars
Poseidon	Neptune	Aphrodite	Venus
Hades	Pluto	Artemis	Diana
Hera	Juno	Hermes	Mercury
Athena	Minerva	Apollo	Apollo

Main Idea and Details

1 What is the main idea of the passage?

a. Zeus and Jupiter were the same gods.
b. The Greek and Roman gods had different names.
c. The Roman gods were stronger than the Greek gods.

2 The Roman god ______ was the same as the Greek god Ares.

a. Mars   b. Mercury   c. Neptune

3 Who was the Roman goddess of wisdom?

a. Juno.   b. Venus.   c. Minerva.

4 What does spread mean?

a. Worshipped.   b. Studied.   c. Passed.

5 Complete the sentences.

a. The Greeks and ______ worshipped the same gods.
b. The Greek god ______ was the Roman god Neptune.
c. The god ______ had the same name in Greece and Rome.

6 Complete the outline.

Gods and Goddesses

Greek Culture

- Spread to many places
- Spread to ancient Rome
- Greek gods were also worshipped by the [a]______.

Greek and Roman Gods and Goddesses

- Zeus = Jupiter
- Hades = Pluto
- Athena = Minerva
- Aphrodite = [d]______
- Hermes = Mercury
- Poseidon = [b]______
- Hera = Juno
- Ares = [c]______
- Artemis = Diana
- Apollo = Apollo

Vocabulary Builder

Write the correct word and the meaning in Chinese.

1 
to show respect for a god

______

2 
the Roman goddess of the hunt

______

3 
the Roman god who was the messenger of the gods

______

4 
the Roman god of light

______

Unit 32

Myths From Ancient Rome

Cupid and Psyche

Key Words

- jealous
- shoot
- arrow
- fall in love
- ugly
- bow
- fly down
- take aim
- slip
- prick
- get married
- curious
- awake
- trust
- depart
- fly away

Once there was a beautiful woman named Psyche. Some people said she was more beautiful than Venus, the goddess of love and beauty.

Venus was jealous, so she said to her son Cupid, "Shoot the girl with your arrow and make her fall in love with the ugliest man on Earth."

Cupid took his bow and arrow and flew down to Earth. Just as he was taking aim to shoot Psyche, his finger slipped. He got pricked with his own arrow and fell in love with Psyche.

They got married. But Cupid came to Psyche only while she slept. He stayed all night, but left before morning's light. One night, Psyche asked Cupid why he came in darkness. "Why should you wish to see me?" he answered. "I love you, and all I ask is that you love me."

Still, Psyche was so curious who her husband was. So, one night Psyche waited until Cupid fell asleep. She lit a lamp and saw the lovely face of Cupid. But a drop of hot oil fell from the lamp and awoke Cupid.

"I asked only for your trust," he said sadly. "When trust is gone, love must depart." And Cupid flew away.

Main Idea and Details

1 What is the passage mainly about?

a. Cupid and Venus. b. Venus and her jealousy.
c. The story of Cupid and Psyche.

2 Venus asked Cupid to shoot Psyche with his __________.

a. arrow b. spear c. gun

3 Why did Cupid fall in love with Psyche?

a. She was so beautiful. b. He got pricked by his own arrow.
c. She was kind and generous.

4 What does wish mean?

a. Demand. b. Desire. c. Depart.

5 According to the passage, which statement is true?

a. Psyche was jealous of Venus.
b. Venus was the mother of Psyche.
c. Psyche got married to Cupid.

6 Complete the outline.

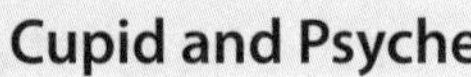

Cupid and Psyche

Cupid

- Was the son of Venus
- Was supposed to make Psyche fall in love with the [a] ________ man on Earth
- Fell in love with [b] ________

Psyche

- Married Cupid
- Could never see his face
- Decided to look at his [c] ________
- Was discovered by Cupid
- Was left by [d] ________

Vocabulary Builder

Write the correct word and the meaning in Chinese.

1 
having a desire to find out about something
____

2 
to target
____

3 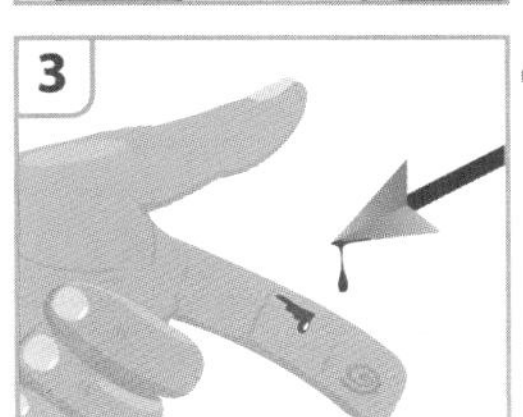
to pierce with a sharp point
____

4 
to go away
____

Vocabulary Review 8

A **Complete the sentences with the words below.**

monsters	demigods	bull	snakes
punished	normal	heavens	Mount Olympus

1 The ancient Greeks believed the gods and goddesses lived on __________ __________.

2 In Greek myths, the gods and goddesses often acted like __________ people.

3 Zeus was the king of the gods and ruled the __________.

4 Greek mythology had many Titans, heroes, and __________ as well as gods.

5 The gods __________ Atlas by making him hold the world up on his shoulders.

6 Greek myths had many heroes, too. These heroes were often __________.

7 Medusa had a woman's head but __________ for hair.

8 The Minotaur was a man with the head of a ________.

B **Complete the sentences with the words below.**

curious	spread	Psyche	fell in love
Roman	Venus	Cupid	worshipped

1 The ancient Greeks __________ their culture to many other places.

2 The gods and goddesses of the ancient Greeks were also __________ by the people of ancient Rome.

3 In __________ mythology, Athena, the goddess of wisdom, became Minerva.

4 Aphrodite, the goddess of love and beauty, became __________.

5 Once there was a beautiful woman named __________.

6 __________ took his bow and arrow and flew down to Earth.

7 Cupid got pricked with his own arrow and ______ _____ ________ with Psyche.

8 Still, Psyche was so __________ who her husband was.

C Write the correct word and the meaning in Chinese.

1 living forever and never dying

____

2 someone who takes messages to other people

____

3 the Roman goddess of love and beauty

____

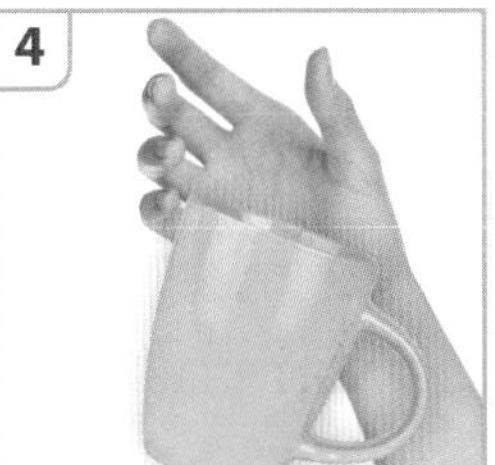

4 to fall from your hands; to fall from position

____

5 a monster that had a woman's head but snakes for hair

____

6 a monster that had the head of a bull

____

D Match each word with the correct definition and write the meaning in Chinese.

1 normal ______________ ☐

2 immortal ______________ ☐

3 Titan ______________ ☐

4 demigod ______________ ☐

5 worship ______________ ☐

6 Mercury ______________ ☐

7 Pluto ______________ ☐

8 take aim ______________ ☐

9 prick ______________ ☐

10 awake ______________ ☐

a. to target
b. usual and ordinary
c. to show respect for a god
d. to pierce with a sharp point
e. living forever and never dying
f. the Roman god of the underworld
g. a powerful giant that fought the gods
h. to wake up; to make someone to wake up
i. the child of a god or goddess and a human
j. the Roman god who was the messenger of the gods

Unit 33

Visual Arts

Architecture and Architects

Architecture is the art of designing buildings. A person who designs buildings is called an architect.

Key Words

- architecture
- design
- architect
- practical
- symmetrical
- symmetry
- symmetric
- column
- dome
- arch
- curve
- brick
- cement
- concrete

Architects try to design buildings that both look nice and are practical. Typically, they try to make sure that their buildings are symmetrical. If something is symmetrical, it has two halves that are exactly the same size and shape. Symmetry makes buildings look nice. One of the most famous examples of symmetric architecture is the Parthenon from ancient Greece.

Some architects add columns, domes, and arches to their buildings to make them look better. The ancient Greeks designed many beautiful temples, especially ones with columns. A dome is a round-shaped roof. An arch is a structure that is curved at the top.

Architects use all kinds of materials in their designs. They might use wood or bricks. They can also use cement, concrete, stone, steel, and even glass. Thanks to architects, we have a wide variety of buildings that all look different from one another.

Symmetry

Temples with Columns in Ancient Greece

Main Idea and Details

1 What is the main idea of the passage?

a. Architects may make buildings of brick, stone, or glass.
b. Architects believe that their buildings must be symmetrical.
c. Architects use many styles and designs on their buildings.

2 The Parthenon from ancient Greece used ____________ architecture.

a. curved b. arched c. symmetrical

3 What is a dome?

a. A round-shaped roof. b. A column. c. A building made of glass.

4 What does especially mean?

a. Possibly. b. Particularly. c. Perhaps.

5 Answer the questions.

a. Who designs buildings? ____________
b. What does a symmetrical building have? ____________
c. What are some materials that architects use for their buildings? ____________

6 Complete the outline.

Architecture

Designs
- Are designed by [a] ____________
- Should look nice and be practical
- Are symmetrical; Both [b] ________ are the same size and shape.

Materials
- Might use wood and [c] ________
- May also use cement, concrete, stone, steel, and [d] ________

Vocabulary Builder

Write the correct word and the meaning in Chinese.

1 
a tall thick post used for supporting a roof or decorating a building ____________

2 
a person who designs buildings ____________

3 
having two halves that are exactly the same size and shape ____________

4 
a block used for building walls and other structures ____________

Unit 34

Visual Arts

Sculptures and Sculptors

Key Words

- artist
- material
- sculpture
- sculptor
- statue
- incredibly
- tiny
- marble
- clay
- metal

Many artists paint or draw. But some prefer to make things with materials other than paint. Artists who make sculptures are called sculptors.

Sculptures are statues that sculptors make. They can be incredibly tiny, or they can be quite large. Sculptors make many different types of sculptures. Sometimes, they make statues of animals, like horses. Other times, they might make statues of men and women. The *Venus de Milo* is a famous ancient sculpture of Venus. And *David*, by Michelangelo, is one of the most famous sculptures in the world.

To make sculptures, artists use many different types of materials. They often prefer stone. Marble is the most common stone they use. It is a hard, white stone. And it makes beautiful sculptures. Other artists use clay to make sculptures. And some of them even use metal or other types of materials.

Some Famous Sculptures in the World

The *Venus de Milo*

David by Michelangelo

The Thinker by Rodin

Main Idea and Details

1 **What is the passage mainly about?**

a. Sculptures. b. Marble. c. Materials.

2 ***David* was a sculpture made by _______________.**

a. Leonardo da Vinci b. Michelangelo c. Venus de Milo

3 **What stone do sculptors most often use?**

a. Marble. b. Glass. c. Metal.

4 **What does tiny mean?**

a. Very small. b. Medium-sized. c. Very large.

5 **Complete the sentences.**

a. _______________ are people who make sculptures.

b. Some sculptors make _______________ of animals like horses.

c. Stone, clay, and metal are common _______________ for sculptures.

6 **Complete the outline.**

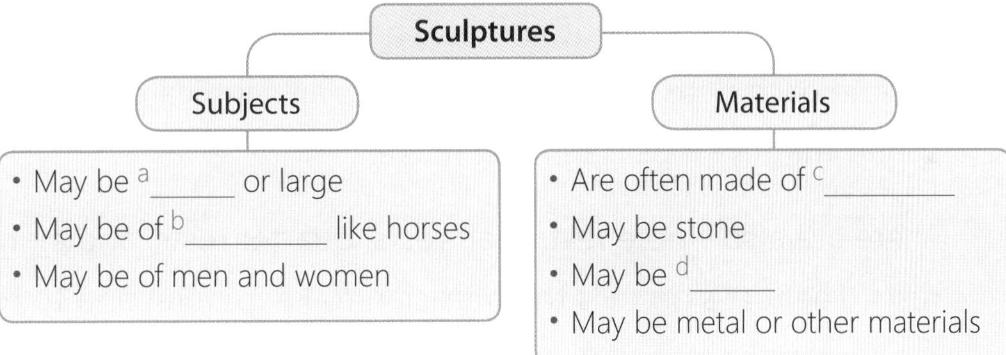

Vocabulary Builder

Write the correct word and the meaning in Chinese.

a work of art that is produced by a sculptor

____

an artist who makes sculptures

____

a hard, usually shiny element that exists naturally in the ground or in rock

____

a hard smooth stone that is usually white with dark lines and is used for building and making statues

____

Unit 35

A World of Music

Elements of Music

Key Words

- musician
- orchestra
- symphony
- conductor
- keep time
- harmony
- (musical) note
- pitch
- staff
- rest
- quarter
- beat

Musicians often play together. They may do this in an orchestra or a symphony. When the musicians play together, they should play the correct music at the same time. If they do not, their music will sound bad. So a conductor leads the musicians. The conductor helps them keep time and play in harmony with one another.

The musicians must be able to read music. Each sound in a piece of music is represented by a musical note. A musical note includes the pitch and length of the musical sound.

Notes are written on a staff. There are whole notes, half notes, quarter notes, and eighth notes. These notes indicate the length of time each note must last. The notes also indicate the type of sound that the musician must make.

There are also whole rests, half rests, quarter rests, and eighth rests. The rest sign tells the musician to keep quiet and to rest during that beat. A whole rest lasts the same amount of time as a whole note. So do the other rests.

Main Idea and Details

1 What is the main idea of the passage?

a. Musicians must read music to play it.
b. All symphonies need a conductor.
c. A rest tells a musician not to play music.

2 There are whole, half, quarter, and ____________ notes.

a. eighth **b.** tenth **c.** twelfth

3 Where do musicians read the notes?

a. In harmony. **b.** By a conductor. **c.** On a staff.

4 What does leads mean?

a. Composes. **b.** Conducts. **c.** Trains.

5 According to the passage, which statement is true?

a. A conductor plays a musical instrument.
b. Musical notes only indicate the pitch.
c. There are both notes and rests on a staff.

6 Complete the outline.

Elements of Music

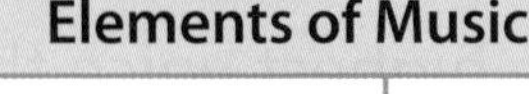

Musicians	Notes	Rests
• Play together in an a__________ or a symphony • The b____________ lets them keep time and play in harmony. • Must read music	• Are written on a staff • Are c________, half, quarter, and eighth notes • Indicate d________ of time of the note • Indicate the type of sound to be made	• Are whole, half, quarter, and eighth rests • Tell the musician to e______

Vocabulary Builder

Write the correct word and the meaning in Chinese.

1

musical notes that are sung or played at the same time to make a pleasant sound

____

2

a set of 5 lines on which music is written

____

3

signs that represent the pitch and length of the musical sound

____

4

the highness or lowness of a sound

____

Unit 36

A World of Music

What's Your Vocal Range?

Key Words

- sound
- vocal range
- tenor
- male
- opera singer
- baritone
- average
- bass
- soprano
- female
- mezzo-soprano
- alto

Men's voices and women's voices sound different from one another. Men and women have a different vocal range.

A person's vocal range is how high and low he or she can sing. A person with a high voice can sing high notes. A person with a low voice can sing low notes. Usually, men's voices are low while women's voices are high.

We can divide men's voices into three categories. Tenor is the highest voice that a male can sing. Many famous opera singers sing tenor. Baritone is an average male voice. Most males sing in the baritone voice. The lowest male voice is called the bass.

As for women, there are three categories for their voices, too. Soprano is the highest voice that a female can sing. Many female opera singers are sopranos. Mezzo-soprano is the average female voice. Most females sing in the mezzo-soprano voice. And alto is the lowest voice that a woman can sing.

✔ Men and women have different vocal ranges.

Main Idea and Details

1 What is the passage mainly about?

a. The vocal range that men and women can sing in.
b. The vocal range that opera singers usually have.
c. Tenors, baritones, and basses.

2 Many male opera singers sing ________.

a. bass **b.** tenor **c.** baritone

3 What is the lowest voice a woman can sing?

a. Alto. **b.** Soprano. **c.** Mezzo-soprano.

4 What does average mean?

a. High. **b.** Range. **c.** Normal.

5 Complete the sentences.

a. A person with a low voice sings low ________.
b. Most males sing ________.
c. Most females sing ________.

6 Complete the outline.

Vocal Ranges

Males' Voices	Females' Voices
• Are usually low	• Are usually [c] ______
• Tenor = highest [a] ______ voice	• Soprano = highest female voice
• Many opera singers are tenors.	• Many opera singers are sopranos.
• Baritone = [b] ______ male voice	• Mezzo-soprano = average female voice
• Bass = lowest male voice	• Alto = [d] ______ female voice

Vocabulary Builder

Write the correct word and the meaning in Chinese.

1 
the range that is how high or low a person can sing

____

2 
the highest male voice

____

3 
the lowest female voice

____

4 
the average female voice

____

Vocabulary Review 9

A **Complete the sentences with the words below.**

columns	architecture	ancient	incredibly
symmetrical	designs	materials	sculptures

1 A person who __________ buildings is called an architect.

2 If something is __________, it has two halves that are exactly the same size and shape.

3 One of the most famous examples of symmetrical __________ is the Parthenon.

4 Some architects add __________, domes, and arches to their buildings.

5 Artists who make __________ are called sculptors.

6 Sculptures can be __________ tiny, or they can be quite large.

7 The *Venus de Milo* is a famous __________ sculpture of Venus.

8 To make sculptures, artists use many different types of __________.

B **Complete the sentences with the words below.**

in harmony	how	represented	female
vocal range	rest sign	musicians	baritone

1 When the __________ play together, they should play the correct music at the same time.

2 The conductor helps the musicians keep time and play _____ __________ with one another.

3 Each sound in a piece of music is __________ by a musical note.

4 The _______ _______ tells the musician to keep quiet and to rest during that beat.

5 Men and women have a different _______ _______.

6 A person's vocal range is _______ high and low he or she can sing.

7 Most males sing in the __________ voice.

8 Soprano is the highest voice that a __________ can sing.

C Write the correct word and the meaning in Chinese.

1

the art of designing buildings

____

2

having two halves that are exactly the same size and shape

____

3

a structure that is curved at the top

____

4

a sculpture of a person or an animal made of stone or metal

____

5

to perform music at the correct speed

____

6

the lowest male voice

____

D Match each word with the correct definition and write the meaning in Chinese.

1 architect ______________ ☐
2 sculpture ______________ ☐
3 sculptor ______________ ☐
4 incredibly ______________ ☐
5 keep time ______________ ☐
6 staff ______________ ☐
7 vocal range ______________ ☐
8 female ______________ ☐
9 bass ______________ ☐
10 mezzo-soprano ______________ ☐

a. a woman
b. to keep the beat
c. the lowest male voice
d. unbelievably; extremely
e. the average female voice
f. a person who designs buildings
g. an artist who makes sculptures
h. a set of 5 lines on which music is written
i. a work of art that is produced by a sculptor
j. the range that is how high or low a person can sing

Wrap-Up Test 3

A Write the correct word for each sentence.

Mount Olympus	sculptors	vertical line	Titans	vocal range
fell in love	endpoints	based on	worshipped	parallel lines

1 A line can go on endlessly, but a line segment has two ____________.

2 When a horizontal line and a __________ ________ intersect, they might form a right angle.

3 If two lines run side by side and never meet, they are __________ ________.

4 The metric system is _________ ______ units of ten.

5 The ancient Greeks believed the gods and goddesses lived on __________ __________.

6 Greek mythology had many ________, heroes, and monsters as well as gods.

7 The gods and goddesses of the ancient Greeks were also ______________ by the people of ancient Rome.

8 Cupid got pricked with his own arrow and ______ _____ ________ with Psyche.

9 Sculptures are statues that ____________ make.

10 A person's ________ _________ is how high and low he or she can sing.

B Write the meanings of the words in Chinese.

1 polygon ____________

2 right angle ____________

3 acute angle ____________

4 perpendicular lines ____________

5 intersect ____________

6 line segment ____________

7 metric system ____________

8 capacity ____________

9 word problem ____________

10 project ____________

11 normal ____________

12 immortal ____________

13 Titan ____________

14 demigod ____________

15 worship ____________

16 Mercury ____________

17 Pluto ____________

18 take aim ____________

19 prick ____________

20 awake ____________

21 magical power ____________

22 architecture ____________

23 symmetrical ____________

24 statue ____________

25 (musical) note ____________

26 rest ____________

27 sculpture ____________

28 incredibly ____________

29 keep time ____________

30 staff ____________

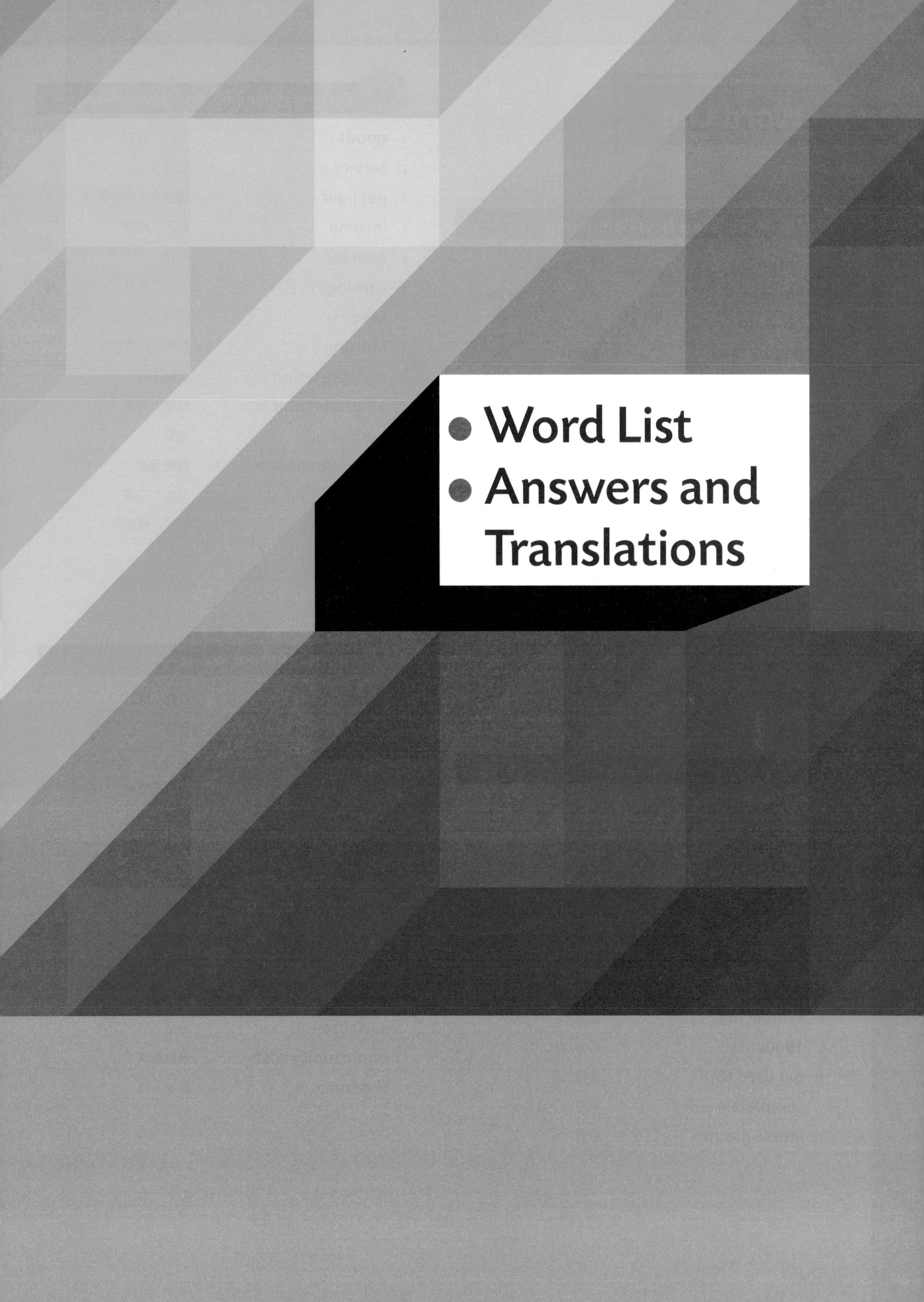
Word List
Answers and Translations

Word List

01 Moving to a New Community

1 **entire** (a.) 全部的；整個的
2 **life** (n.) 生命；人生 *pl. lives
3 **grow up** 成長
4 **nearby** (a.) 附近的
5 **immigrant** (n.) 移民
6 **look for** 尋找
7 **opportunity** (n.) 機會
8 **improve** (v.) 改進；改善
9 **seek** (v.) 尋找；追求 * 動詞三態 seek–sought–sought
10 **freedom** (n.) 自由
11 **education** (n.) 教育
12 **make friends** 交朋友
13 **obey** (v.) 服從；遵守
14 **so that** 以便

02 A Nation of Immigrants

1 **a nation of immigrants** 移民國家
2 **immigrate** (v.) 遷移；遷入
3 **1900s** (n.) 1900 年代
4 **sail** (v.) 航行
5 **Atlantic Ocean** 大西洋
6 **Statue of Liberty** 自由女神像
7 **greet** (v.) 問候；迎接
8 **symbol** (n.) 象徵
9 **1960s** (n.) 1960 年代
10 **get used to** 習慣於
11 **completely** (adv.) 完整地；完全地
12 **ethnic group** 族群

03 Earning, Spending, and Saving Money

1 **goods** (n.) 商品；貨物
2 **service** (n.) 服務
3 **get paid** 領薪水；獲得薪資
4 **income** (n.) 收入；所得
5 **earn** (v.) 賺得
6 **earnings** (n.) 收入；薪資
7 **save** (v.) 儲蓄
8 **housing** (n.) 房屋、住房總稱
9 **transportation** (n.) 運輸工具
10 **entertainment** (n.) 娛樂；消遣
11 **budget** (n.) 預算
12 **make a budget** 編列預算
13 **spending** (n.) 開銷；花費
14 **savings** (n.) 存款；積蓄
15 **balance** (v.) 使平衡
16 **deposit** (v.) 存款（於銀行）

04 Our Needs and Wants

1 **debt** (n.) 債務；借款
2 **go into debt** 負債
3 **avoid** (v.) 避免
4 **carefully** (adv.) 小心謹慎地；仔細地
5 **category** (n.) 種類；類型
6 **needs** (n.) 需求
7 **wants** (n.) 欲求
8 **desire** (v.) 渴望
9 **in order to** 為了
10 **entertainment** (n.) 娛樂；消遣
11 **eat out** 外出用餐
12 **socialize** (v.) 社交
13 **opportunity cost** 機會成本
14 **economic** (a.) 經濟上的

05 World Climate Regions

1 **planet** (n.) 行星
2 **diverse** (a.) 多樣的
3 **climate** (n.) 氣候
4 **refer to** 指的是
5 **major** (a.) 主要的；重要的
6 **tropical climate** 熱帶氣候
7 **temperate climate** 溫帶氣候
8 **polar climate** 寒帶氣候
9 **all year round** 全年；一年到頭
10 **equator** (n.) 赤道
11 **Antarctica** (n.) 南極洲
12 **experience** (v.) 經歷；體驗
13 **distinct** (a.) 有區別的；明顯的
14 **woodland** (n.) 林地
15 **prairie** (n.) 大草原
16 **broadleaf forest** 闊葉林
17 **needleleaf forest** 針葉林
18 **evergreen** (n.) 常綠樹

06 Extreme Weather Conditions

1 **normal** (a.) 正常的；標準的
2 **violent** (a.) 強烈的；劇烈的
3 **extreme** (a.) 極端的；激烈的
4 **except for** 除了⋯⋯之外
5 **blizzard** (n.) 暴風雪
6 **tropical storm** 熱帶風暴
7 **thunder** (n.) 雷；雷聲
8 **lightning** (n.) 閃電
9 **hurricane** (n.) 颶風
10 **typhoon** (n.) 颱風
11 **tornado** (n.) 龍捲風
12 **twister** (n.) 旋風；龍捲風
13 **extremely** (adv.) 極端地；激烈地
14 **damage** (n.) 破壞
15 **drought** (n.) 乾旱
16 **natural hazard** 自然災害；天然災害

17 **monsoon** (n.) 雨季
18 **blow away** 吹散；隨風而去

07 Goods and Resources

1 **natural resource** 自然資源
2 **pump** (v.) 用幫浦抽出
3 **mineral** (n.) 礦物
4 **renewable** (a.) 可再生的；可更新的
5 **nonrenewable** (a.) 不可再生的；不可更新的
6 **solar power** 太陽能
7 **wind power** 風力
8 **replace** (v.) 取代；恢復
9 **opposite** (a.) 相反的
10 **limit** (v.) 限制
11 **be limited in** 對於⋯⋯是有限的
12 **supply** (n.) 供給；供應
13 **conserve** (v.) 保存；保護
14 **run out of** 將⋯⋯用完

08 Goods and Services

1 **factory** (n.) 工廠
2 **crop** (n.) 農作物；莊稼
3 **customer** (n.) 顧客
4 **sale** (n.) 賣；出售
5 **producer** (n.) 生產者；製造者
6 **purchase** (n.) 買；購買
7 **consumer** (n.) 消費者
8 **travel agent** 旅行社職員
9 **product** (n.) 產品；產物
10 **profit** (n.) 利潤；收益
11 **cost** (n.) (v.) 費用；成本；花費
12 **be paid** 被支付 ＊動詞三態 pay–paid–paid

09 American State and Local Governments

1 **several** (a.) 幾個的；數個的
2 **local government** 地方政府
3 **state government** 州政府
4 **federal government** 聯邦政府
5 **be responsible for** 對……應負責任的；對……有責任的
6 **take care of** 照顧
7 **fire department** 消防局
8 **police department** 警察局
9 **govern** (v.) 統治；管理
10 **be based in** 根基於……之內（……表地點、場所、位置）
11 **state capital** 州府
12 **enforce** (v.) 實施；執行
13 **be in charge of** 負責
14 **security** (n.) 安全；防護
15 **infrastructure** (n.) 公共建設
16 **interstate** (n.) 州際公路

10 The Three Branches of Government

1 **Constitution** (n.) 美國憲法
2 **divide (into)** (v.) 分；分割
3 **separate** (a.) 獨立的；單獨的
4 **branch** (n.) 分部；部門
5 **executive branch** 行政部門
6 **legislative branch** 立法部門
7 **judicial branch** 司法部門
8 **duty** (n.) 本分；義務
9 **responsibility** (n.) 責任
10 **Department of Defense** 國防部
11 **carry out** 進行；實行；執行
12 **Congress** (n.) 議會；國會
13 **the Senate** （美）參議院
14 **the House of Representatives** （美）眾議院
15 **role** (n.) 任務；作用；職責
16 **court system** 法院制度
17 **Supreme Court** 最高法院
18 **break the law** 違反法律

11 Laws and Rules

1 **right** (n.) 權利
2 **freedom of speech** 言論自由
3 **freedom of religion** 宗教自由
4 **freedom of the press** 新聞自由
5 **unfortunately** (adv.) 不幸地
6 **court** (n.) 法庭；法院
7 **guilty** (a.) 有罪的
8 **get punished** 受到懲罰
9 **punishment** (n.) 處罰；懲罰
10 **pay a fine** 繳交罰款
11 **community service** （罪犯為避免蹲監獄而從事的）社區服務
12 **crime** (n.) 罪；罪行
13 **in jail** 入獄
14 **severe** (a.) 嚴重的
15 **murder** (n.) 謀殺；謀殺案
16 **case** (n.) 案件；訴訟
17 **lifetime prison sentence** 終生監禁；無期徒刑
18 **death penalty** 死刑

12 The Jury System

1 **trial** (n.) 審問；審判
2 **jury** (n.) 陪審團
3 **regular** (a.) 普通的；一般的
4 **be made up of** 由……所組成
5 **be formed of** 由……所構成
6 **grand jury** 大陪審團
7 **petit jury** 小陪審團
8 **evidence** (n.) 證據
9 **vote to** 投票表決
10 **vote against** 投票反對
11 **criminal case** 刑事案件
12 **prosecutor** (n.) 檢察官

13 **defendant** (n.) 被告
14 **judge** (n.) 法官
15 **proceed** (v.) 繼續進行
16 **smoothly** (adv.) 平穩地；順利地
17 **at the end of** 在……的末尾
18 **verdict** (n.) （陪審團的）裁定；裁決

13 Kinds of Plants

1 **species** (n.) 種類 *pl. species*
2 **flowering plant** 開花植物
3 **conifer** (n.) 針葉植物；針葉樹
4 **reproduce** (v.) 繁殖；生殖
5 **pea** (n.) 碗豆
6 **cone** (n.) 毬果；松果
7 **pine tree** 松樹
8 **fir tree** 冷杉
9 **spruce tree** 雲杉
10 **evergreen tree** 常綠樹
11 **needle** (n.) 針葉
12 **instead of** 代替
13 **deciduous tree** 落葉樹
14 **grow back** 長出來

14 How Do Plants Make Food?

1 **process** (n.) 過程
2 **photosynthesis** (n.) 光合作用
3 **in order to** 為了
4 **substance** (n.) 物質
5 **chlorophyll** (n.) 葉綠素
6 **chloroplast** (n.) 葉綠體
7 **carbon dioxide** 二氧化碳
8 **sugar** (n.) 糖
9 **occur** (v.) 發生（= happen）
10 **take in** 接受；吸收（= absorb）
11 **give off** 發出；散出（= release）
12 **breathe** (v.) 呼吸；呼氣；吸氣

15 Classifications of Animals

1 **according to** 根據；按照
2 **trait** (n.) 特徵；特點
3 **classify** (v.) 將……分類
4 **backbone** (n.) 脊骨；脊柱
5 **vertebrate** (n.) 脊椎動物
6 **reptile** (n.) 爬蟲類動物
7 **invertebrate** (n.) 無脊椎動物
8 **flatworm** (n.) 扁蟲
9 **sponge** (n.) （海中動物）海綿
10 **further** (adv.) 進一步地
11 **warm-blooded** (a.) （動物）溫血的；恆溫的
12 **cold-blooded** (a.) （動物）冷血的
13 **regulate** (v.) 調節；控制
14 **surrounding** (n.) 環境
15 **soak up** 吸收
16 **amphibian** (n.) 兩棲動物

16 What Do Animals Need to Live and Grow?

1 **basic** (a.) 基本的；基礎的
2 **shelter** (n.) 棲身處；避難所
3 **stay alive** 活著；生存（= survive）
4 **run** (v.) 運轉
* 動詞三態
run–ran–run
5 **through** (prep.) 經由；透過
6 **lung** (n.) 肺
7 **instead** (adv.) 作為替代
8 **gill** (n.) 鰓
9 **respond to** 對……作出反應
10 **migrate** (v.) 遷移；遷徙
11 **hibernate** (v.) 冬眠
12 **lie** (v.) 躺；臥
* 動詞三態
lie–lay–lain

17 What Makes up a Food Chain?

1 **organism** (n.) 生物；有機體
2 **be connected with** 與……連結
3 **food chain** 食物鏈
4 **dependent upon** 依賴……
5 **for instance** 例如
6 **at bottom of** 在……底部
7 **decompose** (v.) 分解
8 **nutrient** (n.) 營養物
9 **producer** (n.) 生產者
10 **consumer** (n.) 消費者
11 **decomposer** (n.) 分解者
12 **break down** 分解（= decompose）

18 Herbivores, Carnivores, and Omnivores

1 **herbivore** (n.) 草食性動物（= plant eater）
2 **carnivore** (n.) 肉食性動物（= meat eater）
3 **omnivore** (n.) 雜食性動物
4 **as well** 也
5 **prey animal** 被捕食的動物；獵物型動物
6 **predator** (n.) 掠食者；食肉動物
7 **overlap** (v.) 重疊
8 **path** (n.) 小路；小徑
9 **food web** 食物網
10 **connect** (v.) 連接；結合

19 What Are Ecosystems?

1 **environment** (n.) 環境；自然環境
2 **nonliving thing** 非生物
3 **surround** (v.) 圍繞；包圍
4 **depend on** 依賴……
5 **ecosystem** (n.) 生態系統
6 **grassland** (n.) 草原
7 **be made up of** 由……組成
8 **be found** 被找到；被發現
9 **be filled with** 充滿
10 **compete** (v.) 競爭；對抗
11 **constantly** (adv.) 不斷地；時常地
12 **adapt** (v.) 適應

20 Dinosaurs: Extinct but Still Popular

1 **affect** (v.) 影響
2 **have trouble + V-ing** 有……的困難
3 **dinosaur** (n.) 恐龍
4 **herbivore** (n.) 草食性動物
5 **vicious** (a.) 兇惡的
6 **predator** (n.) 掠食者；食肉動物
7 **fierce** (a.) 兇猛的
8 **in packs** 成群
9 **fearsome** (a.) 可怕的
10 **65 million years** 六千五百萬年
11 **die out** 滅絕；漸漸消失
12 **asteroid** (n.) 小行星
13 **completely** (adv.) 完全地；徹底地
14 **become extinct** 絕種；滅絕
15 **endangered** (a.) 瀕臨絕種的
16 **perish** (v.) 消亡；毀滅

21 The Weather

1 **atmosphere** (n.) 大氣
2 **characteristic** (n.) 特徵；特性
3 **temperature** (n.) 溫度
4 **air pressure** 氣壓
5 **degree** (n.) 度
6 **Fahrenheit** (n.) 華氏溫標
7 **Celsius** (n.) 攝氏溫標
8 **force** (n.) 壓力
9 **meteorologist** (n.) 氣象學者
10 **instrument** (n.) 儀器；器具（= equipment）
11 **thermometer** (n.) 溫度計
12 **barometer** (n.) 氣壓計
13 **anemometer** (n.) 風速計
14 **speed of the wind** 風速

22 The Water Cycle

1 **constant** (a.) 固定的；不變的
2 **form** (n.) (v.) 型態；形式；形成
3 **water cycle** 水循環
4 **stage** (n.) 階段；時期
5 **evaporation** (n.) 蒸發
6 **condensation** (n.) 凝結
7 **precipitation** (n.) 降水
8 **evaporate** (v.) 蒸發
9 **water vapor** 水蒸氣
10 **gaseous** (a.) 氣體的；氣態的
11 **condense** (v.) 凝結
12 **water droplet** 小水滴
13 **release** (v.) 釋放
14 **get absorbed** 被吸收
15 **flow into** 流入
16 **body of water** 水域

23 Rocks, Minerals, and Soil

1 **crust** (n.) 地殼
2 **mineral** (n.) 礦物
3 **igneous rock** 火成岩
4 **sedimentary rock** 沉積岩
5 **metamorphic rock** 變質岩
6 **harden** (v.) 變硬；變堅固
7 **granite** (n.) 花崗岩
8 **basalt** (n.) 玄武岩
9 **pebble** (n.) 鵝卵石
10 **be pressed** 受到擠壓
11 **limestone** (n.) 石灰岩
12 **sandstone** (n.) 沙岩
13 **marble** (n.) 大理石
14 **quartz** (n.) 石英
15 **element** (n.) 【化】元素
16 **carbon** (n.) 碳
17 **crystal** (n.) 水晶
18 **bit** (n.) 小片；小塊
19 **silt** (n.) 粉沙；泥沙
20 **humus** (n.) 腐殖質

24 Fossils and Fossil Fuels

1 **woolly mammoth** 長毛象
2 **alive** (a.) 活著的
3 **fossil** (n.) 化石
4 **remains** (n.) 遺體；遺骨
5 **footprint** (n.) 腳印；足跡
6 **impression** (n.) 壓印；印記
7 **amber** (n.) 琥珀
8 **fossil fuel** 化石燃料
9 **extinct** (a.) 絕種的；滅絕的
10 **thanks to** 幸虧；由於

25 Points, Lines, and Line Segments

1 **dot** (n.) 點；圓點
2 **connect** (v.) 連接；連結
3 **point** (n.) 點
4 **go through** 通過；穿過
5 **segment** (n.) 部分；斷片
6 **line segment** 線段
7 **endlessly** (adv.) 無窮地；繼續地
8 **endpoint** (n.) 端點
9 **horizontal line** 水平線
10 **vertical line** 垂直線
11 **diagonal line** 對角線；斜線
12 **intersect** (v.) 相交；交叉
13 **right angle** 直角
14 **perpendicular lines** 垂直線
15 **side by side** 並排
16 **parallel lines** 平行線

26 Polygons

1 **polygon** (n.) 多邊形
2 **closed figure** 封閉形狀
3 **side** (n.) 邊
4 **five-sided** (a.) 五個邊的
5 **pentagon** (n.) 五邊形
6 **hexagon** (n.) 六邊形
7 **octagon** (n.) 八邊形
8 **certain** (a.) 某幾個；某些
9 **angle** (n.) 角度
10 **right angle** 直角
11 **acute angle** 銳角
12 **less than** 小於
13 **obtuse angle** 鈍角
14 **greater than** 大於

27 The U.S. Customary System and the Metric System

1 **length** (n.) 長度
2 **weight** (n.) 重量
3 **capacity** (n.) 容量
4 **measurement system** 度量系統
5 **U.S. customary system** 美制單位系統
6 **metric system** 公制單位系統
7 **be based on** 以……為基礎
8 **unit** (n.) 單位
9 **foot** (n.) 英尺 *pl. feet
10 **inch** (n.) 英寸
11 **pint** (n.) 品脫
12 **quart** (n.) 夸脫

28 Measurement Word Problems

1 **word problem** 應用題
2 **jog** (v.) 慢跑
3 **string** (n.) 線；細繩
4 **project** (n.) 計畫
5 **butcher** (n.) 肉販；屠夫
6 **convenience store** 便利商店
7 **soda** (n.) 汽水
8 **milliliter** (n.) 毫升

29 Gods and Goddesses in Greek Myths

1 **ancient** (a.) 古代的
2 **Greek** (a.) (n.) 希臘的；希臘人
3 **goddess** (n.) 女神
4 **look down** 俯瞰
5 **normal** (a.) 正常的
6 **argue** (v.) 爭吵
7 **fall in love** 戀愛
8 **get married** 結婚
9 **magical power** 魔力；法力
10 **immortal** (a.) 不死的；長生的
11 **the heavens** 天上；眾天神
12 **the underworld** 冥界；地獄
13 **marriage** (n.) 婚姻
14 **messenger** (n.) 信差；使者

30 Titans, Heroes, and Monsters in Greek Myths

1 **mythology** (n.) 神話（= myth）
2 **Titan** (n.) 泰坦
3 **monster** (n.) 怪物；妖怪
4 **as well as** 和；還有
5 **giant** (n.) 巨人
6 **fight** (v.) 打仗；打架
* 動詞三態
fight–fought–fought
7 **lose** (v.) 輸掉
* 動詞三態
lose–lost–lost
8 **hold up** 托住；支撐
9 **demigod** (n.) 半人半神
10 **while** (conj.) 而；然而
11 **Medusa** (n.) 梅杜莎，希臘神話中三個蛇髮女怪之一

12 **Minotaur** (n.) 米諾陶洛斯，希臘神話中人身牛頭的怪物

13 **centaur** (n.) 半人馬，希臘神話中半人半馬的怪物

14 **satyr** (n.) 薩特，希臘神話中半人半羊的森林之神

31 Same Gods, Different Names

1 **spread** (v.) 傳播；散佈
* 動詞三態
spread–spread–spread

2 **Roman Empire** 羅馬帝國

3 **worship** (v.) 信奉；敬神

4 **though** (adv.) 然而；還是

5 **Jupiter** (n.) 朱比特，古羅馬神話的眾神之王，即希臘神話中的宙斯（Zeus）

6 **Neptune** (n.) 涅普頓海神，即希臘神話中的波塞頓（Poseidon）

7 **Pluto** (n.) 普路托冥王，即希臘神話中的哈帝斯（Hades）

8 **Mars** (n.) 馬爾斯戰神，即希臘神話中的阿瑞斯（Ares）

9 **Venus** (n.) 維納斯，掌管美和愛的女神，即希臘神話的愛芙蘿黛蒂（Aphrodite）

10 **Mercury** (n.) 莫丘利，神的信使，即希臘神話中的赫米斯（Hermes）

32 Cupid and Psyche

1 **jealous** (a.) 妒忌的

2 **shoot** (v.) 射中；射傷
* 動詞三態
shoot–shot–shot

3 **arrow** (n.) 箭

4 **ugliest** (a.) 最醜的
*原級–比較級–最高級
ugly（醜的）– uglier（較醜的）– ugliest（最醜的）

5 **bow** (n.) 弓

6 **fly down** 飛下來

7 **take aim** 瞄準

8 **slip** (v.) 滑落；鬆脫

9 **prick** (v.) 刺；扎

10 **darkness** (n.) 漆黑

11 **curious** (a.) 好奇的

12 **fall asleep** 睡著

13 **light** (v.) 點燃；點燈
* 動詞三態
light–lit–lit

14 **drop** (n.) 滴；一滴

15 **awake** (v.) 叫醒
* 動詞三態
awake–awoke/awaked–awoken/awaked

16 **trust** (n.) 信任；信賴

17 **depart** (v.) 離去

18 **fly away** 飛走
* fly 的動詞三態
fly–flew–flown

33 Architecture and Architects

1 **architecture** (n.) 建築學

2 **architect** (n.) 建築師

3 **practical** (a.) 實用的

4 **typically** (adv.) 典型地；一般地

5 **symmetrical** (a.) 對稱的

6 **half** (n.) 一半；二分之一 **pl.* halves

7 **exactly** (adv.) 完全地

8 **symmetry** (n.) 對稱

9 **Parthenon** (n.) 帕特農神殿

10 **column** (n.) 圓柱；柱形物

11 **dome** (n.) 圓蓋；圓屋頂

12 **arch** (n.) 拱形；拱門

13 **temple** (n.) 神殿；廟宇

14 **structure** (n.) 建築；構造

15 **brick** (n.) 磚塊

16 **a wide variety of** 五花八門；各種各樣的

34 Sculptures and Sculptors

1 **paint** (v.) 繪畫
2 **draw** (v.) 畫
* 動詞三態
draw–drew–drawn
3 **prefer** (v.) 偏好
4 **other than** 除了
5 **sculpture** (n.) 雕刻品；雕像
6 **sculptor** (n.) 雕刻家
7 **statue** (n.) 雕像
8 **incredibly** (adv.) 非常；極為
9 **tiny** (a.) 極小的；微小的
10 **quite** (adv.) 很；相當

35 Elements of Music

1 **musician** (n.) 音樂家；演奏家
2 **conductor** (n.) 指揮家
3 **keep time** 合拍
4 **in harmony** 和諧；協調
5 **read music** 讀樂譜
6 **be represented by** 以……表現
7 **(musical) note** (n.) 音符
8 **pitch** (n.) 音高
9 **staff** (n.) 五線譜
10 **whole note** 全音符
11 **half note** 二分音符
12 **quarter note** 四分音符
13 **eighth note** 八分音符
14 **indicate** (v.) 指出；標出
15 **last** (v.) 持續；延續
16 **rest** (n.) 休止符

36 What's Your Vocal Range?

1 **sound** (v.) 聽起來
2 **vocal range** 音域
3 **tenor** (n.) 男高音
4 **male** (n.) (a.) 男性；男性的
5 **opera singer** 歌劇演唱家
6 **baritone** (n.) 男中音
7 **average** (a.) 一般的；中等的
8 **bass** (n.) 男低音
9 **soprano** (n.) 女高音
10 **female** (n.) (a.) 女性；女性的
11 **mezzo-soprano** (n.) 次女高音；女中音
12 **alto** (n.) 女低音

Answers and Translations

01 Moving to a New Community 移居新社區

有些人一輩子都生活在同一個地方，他們在同一個城市或鄉鎮成長、找工作，並在那裡年華老去。

但有些人則會四處遷徙，搬到鄰近的城市或是其他州，甚至到不同的國家，我們稱這些人為移民。

那麼人們為什麼要搬到新社區呢？他們主要是在尋找改善生活的機會。機會是更好的事情發生的機率。人們通常是為自己或子女追求更好的生活而搬家，有些人甚至前往他國追求自由。

那麼人們到了新社區能做些什麼事呢？他們必須找新工作、接受更完善的教育或是交朋友，也會試著融入當地社會。他們也要遵守社區法律，並且尊重其他的人。如此一來，這個社區才能成為適合居住的好地方。

• **Main Idea and Details**

1 **(a)** 2 **(b)** 3 **(b)** 4 **(a)**

5 a. **entire** b. **opportunities** c. **freedom**

6 a. **countries** b. **educations** c. **freedom** d. **laws**

• **Vocabulary Builder**

1 **opportunity** 機會 2 **improve** 改進；改善

3 **education** 教育 4 **immigrant** 移民

02 A Nation of Immigrants 移民的國家

美國是一個移民的國家，人們從世界各地移居到這裡來。

在 1900 年代早期，許多移民來自歐洲。他們乘船橫越大西洋，通常抵達紐約港的埃利斯島。自由女神像在紐約港歡迎他們。對許多移民而言，「自由女神」是他們抵達美國時，首先映入眼簾的事物。對他們而言，它是自由的象徵。

在 1960 年代，許多移民來自亞洲，他們通常來到舊金山灣的天使島。

移居到其他國家並不是件容易的事。移民們為了適應新環境，經常需要展開一段全新的生活。他們必須學習新文化、找新工作和新房子。他們也得學習新的語言。

有些移民會和相同族群的人住在一起。這些同種族的鄰居能夠幫助他們適應新國家。

• **Main Idea and Details**

1 **(b)** 2 **(b)** 3 **(b)** 4 **(c)** 5 **(c)**

6 a. **Europe** b. **Statue of Liberty** c. **Asia** d. **get used**

• **Vocabulary Builder**

1 **culture** 文化 2 **immigrate** 遷移；移居

3 **symbol** 象徵 4 **ethnic group** 族群

03 Earning, Spending, and Saving Money 賺錢、花錢和存錢

我們花錢買商品和服務。人們工作賺錢，這筆錢他們有了收入。人們工作所賺的錢叫做薪資。

人們通常用收入來做兩件事：花費或儲蓄。人們把錢花在各種事物上，包括房子、食物、交通、衣物和娛樂。

多數人會盡量避免入不敷出，因此，他們往往會編列預算。預算是列出收入、支出和存款的計畫表。編列預算來控制開銷很重要，有了預算，人們才能有計畫地購物，並且使收支平衡。

許多人會存錢未雨綢繆。如果沒有儲蓄，需要用錢時將身無分文。人們通常將錢存入銀行。

• **Main Idea and Details**

1 **(c)** 2 **(a)** 3 **(b)** 4 **(a)**

5 a. **They use money to buy goods and services.**
b. **They spend their money on housing, food, transportation, clothes, and entertainment.**
c. **They deposit it in a bank.**

6 a. **save** b. **housing** c. **earn** d. **bank**

• **Vocabulary Builder**

1 **income/earnings** 收入；薪資 2 **balance** 使收支平衡

3 **deposit** 存放（銀行等） 4 **budget** 預算

04 Our Needs and Wants 需求與欲求

有時人們的支出會大於收入，當這種情況發生時，人們就開始負債。多數人會盡量避免負債，因此他們花錢非常小心。

他們將要購買的物品分為兩類：需求與欲求。需求是人們生活的必需品，欲求則是人們渴望擁有，但非生活必需的物品。

需求比欲求重要，因此人們會優先把錢花在需求上面。哪些是需求呢？房子、食物和衣服是三種重要的需求，每個人都需要有得住、有得吃、有得穿。

欲求有哪些呢？娛樂和旅遊是欲求，外食和應酬也是欲求。

人們不能想買什麼就買什麼，經常必須做抉擇，他們必須考慮機會成本。也就是說，如果將錢花在某樣物品上，可能就無法買另一樣物品。機會成本有助於人們做出聰明的經濟選擇。

• **Main Idea and Details**

1 **(b)** 2 **(b)** 3 **(a)** 4 **(a)**

5 a. **debt** b. **needs** c. **wants**

6 a. **must** b. **clothing** c. **entertainment** d. **choices**

• **Vocabulary Builder**

1 **debt** 負債 2 **economic** 經濟的

3 **socialize** 參與社交；交際 4 **opportunity cost** 機會成本

Vocabulary Review 1

A
1 grow up　2 freedom
3 chance　4 respect
5 immigrants　6 the world
7 Liberty　8 Ethnic

B
1 services　2 earnings
3 less　4 spending
5 debt　6 have
7 desire　8 economic

C
1 look for / seek 尋找　2 ethnic group 族群
3 greet 問候；迎接　4 savings 存款；積蓄
5 entertainment 娛樂；消遣　6 housing 房屋；住宅

D
1 機會 e　2 改進；改善 g
3 尋找 a　4 服從；遵守 c
5 移民 b　6 收入；所得 d
7 開銷；花費 i　8 預算 h
9 渴望 f　10 機會成本 j

05 World Climate Regions 全球氣候區域

我們的地球非常廣大而多元，因此擁有許多不同的氣候。氣候是指一個地區的天氣狀態，主要可分為三種：熱帶、溫帶和寒帶氣候。

熱帶氣候終年炎熱，位於赤道附近地區。這些地區經常降下豪雨。熱帶氣候地區往往會出現雨林。

寒帶氣候終年寒冷，這種氣候型態位於南極洲、部分的俄羅斯和加拿大。這些地區會有大量的冰雪。

全球大部分地區都屬於溫帶氣候，這種氣候不會太熱，也不會太冷，並且有明顯的四季之分。溫帶氣候涵蓋許多不同的區域，有乾林地和大草原，有秋天落葉的闊葉林，還有針葉林。針葉林是常綠樹林，到了冬天也不會落葉。

• **Main Idea and Details**

1 (c)　2 (c)　3 (a)　4 (a)　5 (b)
6 a. equator　b. all year　c. Antarctica　d. seasons

• **Vocabulary Builder**

1 equator 赤道　2 broadleaf 闊葉的
3 temperate climate 溫帶氣候　4 prairie 大草原

06 Extreme Weather Conditions 極端天氣型態

一般我們所經歷的是正常天氣情況，但有時天氣可能會變得非常惡劣，這種情況下，人們所遭遇的是極端的天氣型態。

極端天氣可能具有危險性，它有許多不同的類型。

冬天時，有時候雪下得太大，導致視線不清，眼前只有白茫茫的一片，這就是暴風雪。暴風雪會一次降下大量的雪。

熱帶風暴伴隨著強風、暴雨和雷電。颶風和颱風是其中兩種，龍捲風則是另一種形式的暴風雨。龍捲風是一種風速極快的旋風，可能造成慘重的損害。

洪水和乾旱也是天災的一種。熱帶風暴和大量的季風雨常引發洪水。乾旱地區則是很長一段時間不降雨，那裡的植物乾枯，土壤也會受到風蝕。

• **Main Idea and Details**

1 (a)　2 (c)　3 (a)　4 (b)
5 a. They are tropical storms.
b. Tropical storms and heavy monsoon rains can cause a flood.
c. It is a tornado.
6 a. snow　b. typhoons　c. lightning　d. twisters

• **Vocabulary Builder**

1 blizzard 暴風雪　2 natural hazard 自然災害；天然災害
3 drought 乾旱　4 hurricane 颶風

07 Goods and Resources 商品與資源

地球上有很多種天然資源，人們利用這些資源來製造商品。

我們使用樹木建造家園和建築物，用地底抽出的石油提煉燃料和其他日用品。金和鹽等礦物也是非常重要的天然資源。

地球上的資源可分為可再生資源和不可再生資源。

可再生資源能夠不斷重複利用。水、土壤和樹木都屬於可再生資源。同樣地，太陽能和風力也是可再生資源，它們可以在短時間內恢復。

不可再生資源則相反，它們被使用一次就會永久消失。許多能源，例如石油、煤和天然氣，都是不可再生資源，它們的供給有限，並且無法輕易恢復。

我們必須保護我們的天然資源，它們才不會被消耗殆盡。

• **Main Idea and Details**

1 (c)　2 (c)　3 (b)　4 (a)
5 a. pump　b. renewable　c. limited
6 a. again　b. wind power　c. once　d. replaced

• **Vocabulary Builder**

1 renewable resource 可再生資源　2 wind power 風力
3 mineral 礦物　4 conserve 保存；節省

08 Goods and Services 商品與服務

企業和工廠製造汽車、電腦和家具等商品，農夫在土壤上種植莊稼，然後再將這些商品賣給顧客。

商品是製造或種植來販售的物品，蔬菜、書籍和冰淇淋都是商品。製造商品的人或企業是製造者，製造者努力販賣商品給人們，而購買商品的人則稱為消費者。

有些人為他人提供服務，服務生、廚師、旅行社職員，以及公車和計程車司機都屬於服務業。商品和服務合起來就是產品。

大部分的行業靠著製造商品和提供服務賺取利潤。一個企業扣除總成本之後，剩下來的收益就是利潤。那麼，企業如何獲利呢？如果他們以高於成本的價格販售商品，就能夠獲得利潤。

• **Main Idea and Details**

1 (c)　2 (b)　3 (a)　4 (c)　5 (c)

6 a. sale b. consumers/customers
c. travel agents d. costs

• Vocabulary Builder

1 purchase 購買 2 crops 農作物；莊稼
3 producer 生產者；製造者 4 profit 利潤；收益

Vocabulary Review 2

A 1 diverse 2 equator
3 Polar 4 temperate
5 normal 6 at one time
7 lightning 8 hazards

B 1 resources 2 renewable
3 wind power 4 energy
5 goods 6 products
7 profit 8 costs

C 1 needleleaf forest 針葉林 2 monsoon 雨季
3 nonrenewable resource 不可再生資源
4 solar power 太陽能 5 goods 商品
6 crops 農作物；莊稼

D 1 氣候 e 2 溫帶氣候 h
3 有區別的；明顯的 b 4 極端的；激烈的 f
5 天然災害 j 6 雨季 i
7 取代；恢復 c 8 保存；節省 g
9 消費者 a 10 利潤；收益 d

09 American State and Local Governments 美國各州和地方政府

美國有數種政府組織，包括地方政府、州政府和國家政府。

地方政府在鄉鎮、城市和郡裡運作。州政府負責管理州內事務。國家政府也就是聯邦政府，負責管理整個國家。

地方政府為地方社區的人民提供服務，它們主要負責管理學校、消防局和警察局。

州政府管理整個州，它們位於各州的州府。舉例來說，麻薩諸塞州的波士頓、喬治亞州的亞特蘭大就是該州的州府。州政府負責執行州內的法律。

國家政府位於華盛頓哥倫比亞特區，它最重要的責任是維護所有美國人民的安全，同時也負責國家安全。不過國家政府也負責其他事務，它要為國家立法、執法，也要建造公共建設，如州際公路和一般公路。

• Main Idea and Details

1 (b) 2 (c) 3 (b) 4 (c)

5 a. It is responsible for governing the entire country.
b. They are responsible for schools, fire departments, and police departments.
c. It is based in Washington, D.C.

6 a. responsible b. based c. charge d. enforces

• Vocabulary Builder

1 state capital 州府 2 enforce 實施；執行
3 govern 統治；管理 4 infrastructure 公共建設

10 The Three Branches of Government 政府的三大部門

憲法是美國的最高法律，它將政府分為三個獨立部門，分別是行政部門、立法部門和司法部門，每個部門各有不同的職務和責任。

行政部門以總統為首，總統負責實施國家的法律，但他無法單獨完成這項工作，因此有許多人從旁輔佐。聯邦調查局、中央情報局和國防部都隸屬於行政部門，合力執行國家的法律。

立法部門是國會。國會分為兩個院，上議院是參議院，下議院是眾議院。國會的角色是替國家立法。

司法部門就是法院系統。最高法院是國家最高等級的法院，但是全國各地都有許多較低等級的地方法院。這些法院負責裁決人民是否違法。

• Main Idea and Details

1 (b) 2 (b) 3 (a) 4 (a)

5 a. Constitution b. executive c. court

6 a. president b. Department of Defense
c. Lower house d. Supreme Court e. broken

• Vocabulary Builder

1 Constitution 美國憲法 2 the Senate（美）參議院
3 the House of Representatives（美）眾議院 4 court 法院

11 Laws and Rules 法律與法規

每位公民都有許多權利與義務。

憲法解釋了所有美國人民擁有的權利。例如，美國人民有言論、宗教和新聞自由，他們也有許多其他的權利。

然而，美國人民也有許多義務。舉例來說，他們必須遵守國家的所有法律。美國有許多聯邦法律，也有州法和地方法律。

遺憾的是，人民有時會違反法律。人們違法時，經常必須上法院。如果被定罪，可能要受懲。

懲罰的方式有好幾種。小罪行可能必須繳罰款或從事社區服務，嚴重一點可能要坐牢。罪刑重大如謀殺時，有些人則可能被判無期徒刑或死刑。

• Main Idea and Details

1 (a) 2 (b) 3 (b) 4 (c) 5 (a)

6 a. religion b. Break c. fine d. penalty

• Vocabulary Builder

1 fine 罰金；罰款 2 freedom of the press 新聞自由
3 guilty 有罪的 4 lifetime prison sentence 無期徒刑

12 The Jury System 陪審團制度

憲法賦予所有美國人民接受陪審團審判的權利。在美國，陪審團審判是司法系統很重要的一部分。

陪審團由一般公民組成，任何人都可以擔任陪審團，如商人、家庭主婦、醫生或大學生。

陪審團有兩種：大陪審團和小陪審團。

大陪審團通常由 12 到 23 人組成，負責裁決是否有足夠證據進行審判。如果證據足夠，他們會投票召開審判；如果證據不足，他們會投票反對審判，如此一來案件將不會進入審判。

小陪審團負責裁定實際的刑事案件，通常有 12 位成員。小陪審團在審判期間聽取檢察官和被告的說詞。每次審判也會有一位法官，協助案件審理順利。在審判的最後，陪審團做出裁決，裁定被告是否有罪。

• **Main Idea and Details**

1 **(a)** 2 **(b)** 3 **(c)** 4 **(c)**
5 a. **citizens** b. **trial** c. **judge**
6 a. **evidence** b. **trial** c. **criminal** d. **defendant**

• **Vocabulary Builder**

1 **petit jury** 小陪審團 2 **trial** 審判
3 **prosecutor** 檢察官 4 **defendant** 被告

Vocabulary Review 3

A
1 **governments** 2 **communities**
3 **govern** 4 **keeping**
5 **branches** 6 **executive**
7 **Congress's** 8 **judicial**

B
1 **right** 2 **court**
3 **community service** 4 **serious**
5 **Constitution** 6 **regular**
7 **evidence** 8 **trial**

C
1 **federal government** 聯邦政府
2 **infrastructure** 公共建設 3 **judicial branch** 司法部門
4 **murder** 謀殺；謀殺罪 5 **petit jury** 小陪審團
6 **verdict**（陪審團的）裁決；裁定

D
1 行政部門 **e** 2 負責 **b**
3 統治；管理 **f** 4（美）參議院 **d**
5（美）眾議院 **c** 6 罰金；罰款 **h**
7 有罪的 **a** 8 監獄 **j**
9 檢察官 **g** 10（陪審團的）裁定；裁決 **i**

Wrap-Up Test 1

A
1 **seek** 2 **immigrate**
3 **savings** 4 **in order to**
5 **temperate** 6 **Floods**
7 **nonrenewable** 8 **businesses**
9 **local** 10 **justice**

B
1 移民 2 族群
3 問候；迎接 4 娛樂；消遣
5 參與社交；交際 6 改進；改善
7 尋找 8 遷移；遷入
9 預算 10 機會成本
11 針葉林 12 乾旱
13 商品 14 農作物；莊稼
15 寒帶氣候 16 有區別的；明顯的
17 極端的；激烈的 18 自然災害；天然災害
19 雨季 20 取代；恢復
21 司法部門 22 行政部門
23 立法部門 24 美國國會
25 言論自由 26 罰金；罰款
27（罪犯免蹲牢獄而須從事的）社區服務
28 證據 29（陪審團的）裁定；裁決
30 公共建設

13 Kinds of Plants 植物的種類

植物的種類有很多，而科學家將植物分為兩個主要類別：開花植物和針葉植物。

這兩種植物主要的差異在於它們如何產生種子，植物的種子能讓它們繼續繁殖。

開花植物會開花，並由花裡產生種子。大部分的植物都是開花植物，包括豌豆、草莓、櫻桃和玫瑰。

針葉植物不會開花，它們的種子長在毬果裡。松樹、冷杉和雲杉屬於針葉樹。

許多針葉樹都是常綠樹。常綠樹不同的是葉子為針葉，而且終年常綠。

雖然多數針葉樹的葉子為針葉，但是落葉樹仍為樹木的大宗。落葉樹的葉子為闊葉，到了秋天通常會變色。此外，它們到了冬天也會落葉。春天時，葉子又重新生長出來。

• **Main Idea and Details**

1 **(b)** 2 **(c)** 3 **(b)** 4 **(c)**
5 a. **seeds** b. **needles** c. **fall**
6 a. **flowers** b. **cones** c. **pine trees** d. **broad**

• **Vocabulary Builder**

1 **needle** 針葉 2 **deciduous trees** 落葉樹
3 **conifers** 針葉樹 / **evergreen trees** 常綠樹
4 **cone** 毬果；松果

14 How Do Plants Make Food? 植物如何製造食物？

所有生物都需要能量來維持生命。動物靠食物獲取能量，而植物則會自己製造食物，它們透過光合作用的程序來製造食物。

植物利用陽光來製造食物，葉子是它們製造食物的主要部位。

葉子呈現綠色是由於一種叫做葉綠素的物質，葉綠素存在於葉綠體，這也是植物製造食物的地方。

首先，當陽光照射在葉子上，葉綠素會吸收陽光。接著，葉綠體利用二氧化碳、水和陽光的能量來造糖，這個糖就是植物的食物，而此過程叫做光合作用。

當光合作用發生時，植物從空氣中吸收二氧化碳，同時也釋放氧氣到空氣中，這就是人類所呼吸的氧氣。所有動物都必須吸取氧氣以維持生命，因此，人類和動物也因植物而得以生存。

• **Main Idea and Details**

1 **(c)** 2 **(a)** 3 **(c)** 4 **(b)** 5 **(c)**
6 a. **chlorophyll** b. **chloroplasts** c. **absorbs** d. **sugar**

• Vocabulary Builder

1 **photosynthesis** 光合作用　2 **chlorophyll** 葉綠素
3 **breathe** 呼吸　4 **carbon dioxide** 二氧化碳

15 Classifications of Animals 動物的分類

動物可依照其特徵來分類，其中一個分類動物的方式，就是看牠們是否有脊骨。

有脊骨的動物稱為脊椎動物，所有哺乳動物、鳥類、爬蟲類、魚類和兩棲動物，都屬於脊椎動物。

沒有脊骨的動物稱為無脊椎動物，無脊椎動物包括昆蟲、扁蟲、海綿、蝦和龍蝦。

所有脊椎動物可進一步分為兩類：溫血動物和冷血動物。

溫血動物可以自行調節體溫，因此不論外界極冷或極熱，牠們的身體永遠保持恆溫。哺乳動物和鳥類屬於溫血動物。

冷血動物需要陽光為身體保暖，所以牠們的體溫會隨著周遭環境的溫度而變化。這些動物通常會在陽光下休息好幾個小時來吸收熱量。爬蟲類、魚類和兩棲動物都屬於冷血動物。

• Main Idea and Details

1 **(b)**　2 **(b)**　3 **(c)**　4 **(c)**

5 a. **All mammals, birds, reptiles, fish, and amphibians are vertebrates.**
b. **Insects, flatworms, sponges, shrimp, and lobsters are invertebrates.**
c. **Mammals and birds are warm-blooded.**

6 a. **mammals**　b. **backbones**　c. **Warm-blooded**
d. **Cold-blooded**　e. **sun**

• Vocabulary Builder

1 **trait** 特徵；特點　2 **amphibian** 兩棲動物
3 **vertebrate** 脊椎動物　4 **cold-blooded** 冷血的

16 What Do Animals Need to Live and Grow? 動物生長需要什麼？

所有動物皆有生存與成長的基本需求，牠們都需要食物、水、空氣和棲所。

所有動物需要食物和水才能生存，食物和水是牠們的能量來源。就像機器需要燃料來運作，所有的動物也要有能量才能勞動。當動物漸漸成長，牠們也需要更多的食物和水。

所有動物都需要氧氣才能呼吸，牠們如何獲取氧氣呢？陸上動物靠肺來吸取氧氣，但是魚類和一些水生動物沒有肺，而是用鰓來吸取水中的氧氣。

所有動物都需要棲身之處——一個供牠們生活的地方，這個棲所能保護他們免於天氣和其他動物的威脅。

動物也會因應環境變遷以求生存。當天氣變冷，有些動物會遷徙到較溫暖的地方，有些會找地方冬眠。冷血動物則會躺在陽光下取暖。

• Main Idea and Details

1 **(a)**　2 **(a)**　3 **(a)**　4 **(b)**

5 a. **water**　b. **weather**　c. **migrate**

6 a. **grow**　b. **breathe**　c. **gills**　d. **animals**

• Vocabulary Builder

1 **stay alive / survive** 活著；生存　2 **shelter** 棲身處；避難所
3 **migrate** 遷移；遷徙　4 **hibernate** 冬眠

Vocabulary Review 4

A
1 **seeds**　2 **flowers**
3 **cones**　4 **broad leaves**
5 **process**　6 **chlorophyll**
7 **chloroplasts**　8 **carbon dioxide**

B
1 **backbones**　2 **vertebrates**
3 **without**　4 **divided**
5 **needs**　6 **fuel**
7 **keeps**　8 **respond**

C
1 **flowering plants** 開花植物
2 **conifers** 針葉樹 / **evergreen trees** 常綠樹
3 **photosynthesis** 光合作用　4 **chlorophyll** 葉綠素
5 **invertebrate** 無脊椎動物　6 **migrate** 遷移；遷徙

D
1 落葉樹 **h**　2 繁殖；生殖 **i**
3 接受；吸收 **b**　4 發出；散出 **c**
5 特徵；特點 **f**　6 無脊椎動物 **e**
7 調節；控制 **a**　8 活著；生存 **d**
9 遷移；遷徙 **j**　10 冬眠 **g**

17 What Makes up a Food Chain? 食物鏈的組成

動物無法自己製造食物，牠們以其他有機體為食。有些動物吃植物，有些則吃動物。大多數的動物都在食物鏈中互相連結。

食物鏈顯示所有生物如何彼此賴以為食。

譬如說，在食物鏈的底層，植物利用日光自行製造食物，然後可能兔子吃了這株植物，接著可能狐狸吃了這隻兔子，再來可能狼又吃了這隻狐狸，最後狼也死亡，身體腐爛分解，提供土地養分，讓更多植物生長。

地球上所有的生物都是生產者、消費者或分解者。生產者，如植物，能自行製造食物。消費者是食用生產者或其他消費者的生物，動物就是消費者。分解者是分解其他有機體的生物。牠們合起來構成了食物鏈。

• Main Idea and Details

1 **(c)**　2 **(c)**　3 **(a)**　4 **(c)**　5 **(b)**

6 a. **depend**　b. **plants**　c. **consumers**　d. **break**

• Vocabulary Builder

1 **food chain** 食物鏈　2 **producer** 生產者
3 **consumer** 消費者　4 **decompose** 分解

18 Herbivores, Carnivores, and Omnivores 草食性、肉食性和雜食性動物

所有動物都需要飲食才能生存，不同的消費者以不同的食物為食。根據動物所吃的食物，可將牠們分為三類，分別是草食性、肉食性和雜食性動物。

草食性動物只吃植物，我們稱這些動物為食草者。草食性動物有很多種，可能小如兔子，也可能碩大如牛，大象也是草食性動物。這些動物也常被稱為獵物型動物。

肉食性動物是食肉者，牠們通常追捕獵物型動物，也會獵殺其他動物。獅子、老虎和鯊魚都是危險的肉食性動物。肉食性動物常被稱為掠食者。

有些動物吃肉也吃植物，我們稱之為雜食性動物。狼和豬是雜食性動物，人類也屬於雜食性動物。

食物鏈可能重疊，不一定遵循單一路徑。數個重疊的食物鏈構成一個食物網。食物網顯示食物鏈如何相互連結。

- Main Idea and Details

1 **(b)** 2 **(a)** 3 **(a)** 4 **(c)**

5 a. **Herbivores are plant eaters.**
b. **They eat meat.**
c. **They eat meat and vegetation.**

6 a. **plant** b. **elephants** c. **meat**
d. **predators** e. **humans**

- Vocabulary Builder

1 **herbivore** 草食性動物 2 **carnivore** 肉食性動物
3 **omnivore** 雜食性動物 4 **overlap** 重疊

19 What Are Ecosystems? 何謂生態系統？

我們生活在自然環境裡，自然環境是圍繞在我們四周的所有生物和非生物的總稱。

一個環境裡的動植物互相依存，同時也依賴非生物，如水、空氣和土壤。一個區域中的所有生物和非生物，合起來便構成了生態系統。

地球上有許多不同的生態系統，有沙漠、森林、草原、湖泊和海洋生態系統。

不同的生態系統由不同的動植物組成。森林裡有許多樹木和動物，湖泊裡有魚類、青蛙和昆蟲。

這些生態系統內的生物互相競爭以求生存。沙漠植物爭水，掠食者爭奪獵物，獵物型動物如兔子和松鼠則爭採食物。

生態系統隨時都在改變，因此動植物也必須適應這些改變。適者生存，無法適應的生物則被淘汰。

- Main Idea and Details

1 **(c)** 2 **(b)** 3 **(b)** 4 **(c)**

5 a. **All of the living and nonliving things in an area are an environment.**
b. **There are desert, forest, grassland, lake, and ocean ecosystems.**
c. **They must adapt.**

6 a. **nonliving** b. **depend** c. **ocean** d. **adapt**

- Vocabulary Builder

1 **ecosystem** 生態系統 2 **nonliving things** 非生物
3 **compete** 競爭；對抗 4 **collect** 收集；採集

20 Dinosaurs: Extinct but Still Popular 恐龍：已絕種卻仍廣受喜愛

生態系統會改變，當巨大的改變發生時，生態系統裡的生物無不受到影響，有些生物甚至面臨生存危機。

你喜歡恐龍嗎？恐龍在數百萬年前曾經生活在地球上。有些恐龍體型巨大，如雷龍和三角龍，牠們是草食性動物。但是也有很多凶暴的掠食性動物，迅猛龍是團隊合作獵食的兇猛掠食者，暴龍則是全部當中最令人生畏的一種恐龍。

然而，大約在六千五百萬年前，恐龍突然絕跡。科學家認為當時有一顆巨大的小行星撞擊地球，導致地球生態完全改變。地球上的天氣變冷，陽光變少，地球生態系統徹底改變，許多動植物死亡。恐龍也因無法適應環境而絕種，目前地球上已不見恐龍的蹤跡。

甚至到了今日，許多生物仍然瀕臨絕種，如果牠們無法適應環境的改變，部分瀕危的動物可能就會死亡。

- Main Idea and Details

1 **(b)** 2 **(c)** 3 **(a)** 4 **(a)** 5 **(b)**

6 a. **herbivores** b. **predators** c. **million** d. **dinosaurs**

- Vocabulary Builder

1 **asteroid** 小行星 2 **vicious/fierce** 兇惡的；兇猛的
3 **pack**（獵犬、野獸等的）一群
4 **die out / become extinct** 絕種；滅絕

Vocabulary Review 5

A 1 **connected with** 2 **dependent**
3 **organisms** 4 **break down**
5 **according to** 6 **plants**
7 **prey animals** 8 **food chains**

B 1 **environment** 2 **form**
3 **made up of** 4 **compete**
5 **affected** 6 **brontosaurus**
7 **in packs** 8 **extinct**

C 1 **organism** 生物；有機體 2 **adapt** 適應
3 **carnivore** 肉食性動物 4 **prey animal** 獵物型動物
5 **decomposer** 分解者 6 **dinosaur** 恐龍

D 1 生物；有機體 **d** 2 生態系統 **j**
3 分解 **e** 4 依賴 **c**
5 競爭；對抗 **f** 6 適應 **a**
7 掠食者；食肉動物 **h** 8 兇惡的；殘暴的 **i**
9 可怕的；令人生畏的 **g** 10 絕種；滅絕 **b**

21 The Weather 天氣

天氣是大氣的狀態，有三個主要特徵：溫度、氣壓和風。

溫度告訴我們現在多熱或多冷。我們用「度」來測量溫度，而溫標有兩種，分別是華氏溫標和攝氏溫標，華氏 32 度等於攝氏 0 度。

氣壓是空氣中的壓力總量。氣壓低時，可能會下雨或下雪。氣壓高時，通常天氣晴朗。

空氣移動時會產生風。有時候風吹得很強，有時候可能完全無風。

天氣不斷在變化，氣象學家運用許多儀器來測量天氣。三種最重要的儀器分別是溫度計、氣壓計和風速計。溫度計用來測量氣溫，氣壓計測量氣壓，風速計測量風速。

• Main Idea and Details

1 **(c)** 2 **(c)** 3 **(a)** 4 **(a)**

5 a. **They are Fahrenheit and Celsius.**
b. **It may rain or snow.**
c. **It measures the air pressure.**

6 a. **Celsius** b. **Thermometer** c. **air pressure** d. **measures** e. **wind speed**

• Vocabulary Builder

1 **air pressure** 氣壓 2 **atmosphere** 大氣
3 **anemometer** 風速計 4 **Fahrenheit** 華氏溫標

22 The Water Cycle 水循環

地球上的總水量是不變的，然而，這些水可能會改變形態，我們稱這些變化為水循環。

水循環有三個階段：蒸發、凝結和降水。

河川、湖泊和海洋裡有水。水是液體，當太陽照射在水上，陽光的熱度會導致一些水蒸發，因而形成水蒸氣，也就是氣態的水。

水蒸氣上升到大氣中。而在空氣中，隨著高度增加，溫度會下降。於是水蒸氣凝結，再度變為液體。這些小水滴聚集成雲，事實上，雲就是無數的小水滴所組成。有時候，雲變得太重了，就會釋放水分，以雨、雪或冰的形式降到地面。

有些水被地面吸收，但是其他時候則是流入水域，然後水循環再次展開。

• Main Idea and Details

1 **(a)** 2 **(b)** 3 **(a)** 4 **(c)**

5 a. **They are evaporation, condensation, and precipitation.**
b. **Clouds are made of billions of water droplets.**
c. **They are rain, snow, and ice.**

6 a. **heat** b. **gaseous** c. **water droplets** d. **release** e. **flows into**

• Vocabulary Builder

1 **water cycle** 水循環 2 **evaporate** 蒸發
3 **condense** 凝結 4 **body of water** 水域

23 Rocks, Minerals, and Soil 岩石、礦物和土壤

地殼由岩石、礦物和土壤組成，岩石有三大種類：火成岩、沉積岩和變質岩。

火成岩非常堅硬，是由熔岩冷卻凝固而成。花崗岩和玄武岩屬於火成岩。

沉積岩質地較軟，是由層層的沙子、泥土和鵝卵石受到擠壓而成。沉積岩有石灰岩和沙岩。

變質岩是由一種岩石發生改變所形成的岩石。大理石和石英是常見的變質岩。

岩石由多種礦物組成。礦物是自然界中的堅硬物質，它可以是碳、鐵或金等元素，也可以是石英這類的水晶。

土壤由許多不同的物質所構成，包括小石礫和礦物。泥沙、黏土、沙和腐殖質都屬於土壤。我們利用土壤來種植植物。

• Main Idea and Details

1 **(b)** 2 **(c)** 3 **(a)** 4 **(c)** 5 **(a)**

6 a. **melted rocks** b. **pressed** c. **limestone** d. **changed**

• Vocabulary Builder

1 **metamorphic rock** 變質岩 2 **sedimentary rock** 沉積岩
3 **mineral** 礦物 4 **element** 元素

24 Fossils and Fossil Fuels 化石和化石燃料

長毛象曾生活在數千年以前，不過現今已從地球上消失無蹤，恐龍也已滅絕。那麼，我們該如何認識牠們呢？我們透過牠們的化石來認識牠們。

何謂化石？化石是古代動植物死後所留下的遺體，經過漫長的時間才能形成。外殼、牙齒和骨骼都能成為化石。化石甚至可以是岩石上的足跡或壓印。大多數的化石被發現於沉積岩內，有的則被保存在琥珀中。

我們也可以從化石中取得燃料，煤、石油和天然氣皆屬於化石燃料。化石燃料是由很久以前死亡的動植物遺體所形成。

科學家研究化石是為了瞭解地球的種種過去。化石告訴我們地球上的生命如何改變，並且訴說著地球的歷史。也因為化石的存在，我們得以瞭解許多關於絕種動植物的知識。

• Main Idea and Details

1 **(c)** 2 **(a)** 3 **(b)** 4 **(c)**

5 a. **teeth** b. **animals** c. **fossils**

6 a. **bones** b. **amber** c. **natural gas** d. **remains**

• Vocabulary Builder

1 **remains** 遺體；遺骨 2 **fossil fuel** 化石燃料
3 **amber** 琥珀 4 **impression** 壓印；印記

Vocabulary Review 6

A
1 atmosphere　2 Fahrenheit
3 force　4 instruments
5 constant　6 evaporation
7 condenses　8 water droplets

B
1 minerals　2 melted rock
3 Sedimentary　4 changed
5 Woolly mammoths　6 remains
7 fossils　8 Scientists

C
1 water vapor 水蒸氣
2 precipitation 降水；降雨；降雪
3 igneous rock 火成岩　4 barometer 氣壓計
5 fossil 化石　6 humus 腐殖質

D
1 蒸發 b　2 凝結 g
3 氣壓 d　4 氣象學者 e
5 變質岩 i　6 火成岩 f
7 礦物 h　8 變硬；變堅固 a
9 遺體；遺骨 j　10 腳印；足跡 c

Wrap-Up Test 2

A
1 oxygen　2 vertebrates
3 omnivores　4 food chain
5 needles　6 depend on
7 ecosystems　8 condensation
9 soil　10 Fossils

B
1 開花植物　2 針葉植物；針葉樹
3 落葉樹　4 常綠樹
5 接受；吸收　6 發出；散出
7 特徵；特點　8 調節；控制
9 遷移；遷徙　10 冬眠
11 棲身處；避難所　12 光合作用
13 葉綠素　14 葉綠體
15 二氧化碳　16 脊骨；脊柱
17 脊椎動物　18 無脊椎動物
19 溫血動物　20 冷血動物
21 肉食性動物　22 掠食者；食肉動物
23 降水；降雨；降雪　24 壓印；印記
25 蒸發　26 凝結
27 氣象學者　28 沉積岩
29 變質岩　30 火成岩

25 Points, Lines, and Line Segments 點、線和線段

在一張紙上畫一個點，然後再畫另一個點。現在，把這兩點連起來，你就畫出了一條直線，而這兩點則稱為「點」。你可以給這些點命名：A　B 我們稱它們為點 A 和點 B。通過點 A 和 B 的線叫做線 AB，也可以寫成 $\overleftrightarrow{AB}$。

某物的一部分叫做段，而線段就是線的一部分。C　D 線可以無止盡延伸，但是線段卻有兩個端點，我們用線段的端點來為它命名，例如：線段 CD 或 $\overline{CD}$。

線有許多不同的方向，從左到右的是水平線，由上到下的是垂直線，成一個角度的是斜線。

有時候兩條線會交叉，我們可以說這兩條線相交。水平線和垂直線相交時，可能會形成一個直角，成直角的兩條線叫做垂直線。兩條並列並且永不相交的線叫做平行線。

- **Main Idea and Details**

1 (a)　2 (b)　3 (a)　4 (c)
5 a. angle　b. form　c. Parallel
6 a. endpoints　b. endlessly　c. Diagonal line　d. side by side

- **Vocabulary Builder**

1 intersect 相交；交叉　2 line segment 線段
3 parallel lines 平行線　4 horizontal line 水平線

26 Polygons 多邊形

多邊形有很多種。多邊形由三條以上的線段組成，並且必須是一個封閉圖形，意思就是說，多邊形的所有線條必須相交。

三個邊的多邊形是三角形，四個邊的多邊形是正方形或長方形，五個邊的是五邊形，六個邊叫六邊形，八個邊叫八邊形。

當我們創造一個多邊形時，所有線條會在某個點交會。兩條線相交時，會構成一個角度。

舉例來說，正方形有四個邊，因此會有四個角，每個角都是直角，也就是說每個角都是 90 度。但是並非所有多邊形都有直角，有的多邊形有銳角，也就是小於 90 度的角。有些多邊形有大於 90 度的鈍角。

- **Main Idea and Details**

1 (a)　2 (c)　3 (c)　4 (a)　5 (c)
6 a. closed　b. line segments　c. Hexagon　d. obtuse angles

- **Vocabulary Builder**

1 polygon 多邊形　2 octagon 八邊形
3 right angle 直角　4 obtuse angle 鈍角

27 The U.S. Customary System and the Metric System 美制和公制單位系統

我們經常需要知道各種物品的長度、重量和容量，我們用度量系統來測量它們。兩大度量系統分別是:美制和公制單位系統。

美制系統用於美國，全世界多用公制系統。公制以十進位為基礎，美制則使用不同的度量方法。

公制使用公尺來測量長度，小一點的單位有公分和公釐，大一點的單位有公里。美制用英尺，一英尺有 12 英寸，大一點的單位則用英里。

公制使用公克和公斤來測量重量。美制則用盎司和磅，一磅等於 16 盎司。

公制使用公升來測量容量。美制則用杯、品脫、夸脫和加侖。

• Main Idea and Details

1 (b) 2 (b) 3 (a) 4 (c)

5 a. **Most of the world uses the metric system.**
b. **One foot is 12 inches.**
c. **It is the liter.**

6 a. **inch** b. **Weight** c. **meter** d. **Capacity**

• Vocabulary Builder

1 **U.S. customary system** 美制系統 2 **metric system** 公制系統
3 **capacity** 容量 4 **weight** 重量

28 Measurement Word Problems 測量應用題

❶ 約翰喜歡慢跑，他早上會跑 700 公尺，下午跑 1,200 公尺，傍晚跑 800 公尺，他一天總共跑了幾公里？

⇨ 他總共跑了 2,700 公尺，而一公里等於 1,000 公尺，2700 ÷ 1000 = 2.7 ，因此他總共跑了 2.7 公里。

❷ 莎莉正在為一個科學計畫剪繩子，她需要 7 英尺的繩子，但是她的尺只能測量英寸，她需要多少英寸的繩子呢？

⇨ 1 英尺等於 12 英寸，7 × 12 = 84 ，所以她需要 84 英寸的繩子。

❸ 詹姆士到店裡買火腿，他要肉販給他一磅半的火腿，他會拿到幾盎司的火腿呢？

⇨ 一磅等於 16 盎司，1.5 × 16 = 24 ，他買到 24 盎司的火腿。

❹ 黛安娜因為口渴到便利商店買飲料，她買了 500 毫升的罐裝汽水，她買了幾公升的汽水呢？

⇨ 1 公升等於 1,000 毫升，500 ÷ 1000 = 0.5 ，她買了 0.5 公升的汽水。

• Main Idea and Details

1 (b) 2 (b) 3 (a) 4 (a)

5 a. **foot** b. **ounces** c. **liter**

• Vocabulary Builder

1 **word problem** 應用題 2 **jog** 慢跑
3 **total** 總數；合計 4 **butcher** 肉販；屠夫
5 **convenience store** 便利商店 6 **thirsty** 口渴的

Vocabulary Review 7

A 1 **points** 2 **line segment**
3 **perpendicular** 4 **parallel**
5 **intersect** 6 **polygon**
7 **octagon** 8 **obtuse**

B 1 **weight** 2 **customary**
3 **based on** 4 **measure**
5 **kilogram** 6 **pound**
7 **capacity** 8 **milliliters**

C 1 **pentagon** 五邊形 2 **acute angle** 銳角
3 **total** 總數；合計 4 **line segment** 線段
5 **diagonal line** 對角線；斜線 6 **metric system** 公制單位系統

D 1 多邊形 **h** 2 銳角 **c**
3 垂直線 **g** 4 美制單位系統 **d**
5 容量 **b** 6 單位 **i**
7 應用題 **f** 8 慢跑 **a**
9 計畫 **e** 10 便利商店 **j**

29 Gods and Goddesses in Greek Myths 希臘神話中的男女眾神

古希臘人相信有許多男女天神的存在，他們相信眾神住在希臘最高的奧林帕斯山上，從這裡俯瞰人間，主宰人類和大自然。

在希臘神話裡，眾神們的行為常與一般人無異，祂們要飲食、睡覺，也會爭吵、相愛和結婚。然而，祂們擁有法力和不死之身，永遠不會死亡。

宙斯是權力最高的天神，祂是眾神之王，統治眾天神。祂的兄弟波塞頓是海神，另一個兄弟則是冥王哈帝斯。

赫拉是宙斯的妻子，也是婚姻女神。雅典娜是智慧女神；阿瑞斯是戰神；愛芙蘿黛蒂是愛與美之女神；赫米斯是神使；阿波羅是宙斯的兒子，也是光明之神，他的孿生妹妹阿提密斯是狩獵女神。

• Main Idea and Details

1 (c) 2 (a) 3 (b) 4 (b) 5 (a)

6 a. **Mount Olympus** b. **immortal** c. **Poseidon**
d. **Athena** e. **Apollo**

• Vocabulary Builder

1 **the underworld** 冥界 2 **magical power** 魔力；法力
3 **immortal** 不死的；長生的 4 **twin** 孿生的

30 Titans, Heroes, and Monsters in Greek Myths 希臘神話中的泰坦、英雄和怪物

希臘神話裡有許多泰坦、英雄、怪物和天神。

泰坦是具有神力的巨人，曾經大戰天神卻落敗。阿特拉斯是最強壯的泰坦，天神為了懲罰祂，命令祂用肩膀支撐世界。普羅米修斯也是一個泰坦，祂從眾神那裡偷火給地球上的人類。

希臘神話中也有許多英雄人物，這些英雄通常是半人半神，是神和人所生的後代。海克力斯是其中最偉大的英雄，他是宙斯之子，也是世界上最強壯的人。帕修斯、特修斯、阿基里斯和奧德修斯都是英雄。

最後，還有許多怪物，瑪杜莎有著女人頭和蛇髮，任何人只要看她一眼，就會變成石頭。米諾陶洛斯是有著牛頭的人；半人馬是半人半馬的怪物；薩特是半人半羊。

• Main Idea and Details

1 (c) 2 (a) 3 (b) 4 (a)

5 a. **He stole fire from the gods and gave it to man.**
b. **Atlas was the strongest Titan.**
c. **It was half man and half goat.**

6 a. **giants** b. **shoulders** c. **Heracles** d. **stone** e. **Satyr**

• Vocabulary Builder

1 Titan 泰坦　　2 demigod 半人半神
3 centaur 半人馬　　4 satyr 薩特

31 Same Gods, Different Names 同神不同名

古希臘人將他們的文化傳播到其他許多地方，羅馬帝國是其中之一，古羅馬人也同樣信奉古希臘的男女眾神。

然而羅馬人並不沿用希臘的神祇名稱，而是替祂們重新命名。

宙斯是希臘神話裡的眾神之王，但是在羅馬神話裡，祂的名字叫做朱比特。波塞頓是希臘的海神，羅馬名卻是涅普頓。哈帝斯是希臘的冥界之神，但羅馬人稱祂為普路托。

其他眾神也有新的名字。宙斯的妻子赫拉變成朱諾；智慧女神雅典娜變成米娜娃；戰神阿瑞斯變成馬爾斯；愛與美之女神愛芙蘿黛蒂變成維納斯；狩獵女神阿提密斯改稱黛安娜；神之信使赫米斯成了莫丘利。然而光明之神阿波羅還是叫做阿波羅。

• Main Idea and Details

1 (b)　2 (a)　3 (c)　4 (c)
5 a. Romans　b. Poseidon　c. Apollo
6 a. Romans　b. Neptune　c. Mars　d. Venus

• Vocabulary Builder

1 worship 信奉；敬神　　2 Diana 黛安娜，狩獵女神
3 Mercury 莫丘利，神的信使　　4 Apollo 阿波羅；光明之神

32 Cupid and Psyche 邱比特與賽姬

從前有一位美人叫做賽姬，有人說她的美麗更勝掌管愛和美之女神維納斯。

維納斯心生妒忌，於是對祂的兒子丘比特說：「用你的箭射向這名女子，讓她愛上全世界最醜陋的男人。」

丘比特帶著祂的弓箭飛到人間，就在他瞄準賽姬時，手指一滑，被自己的箭刺傷，就此愛上了賽姬。

他倆於是結婚，但是丘比特只在賽姬熟睡時才去找她。祂會整晚陪著賽姬，卻在破曉前就離開。有一晚，賽姬問丘比特為何只在晚上出現。丘比特答道：「為什麼你想看到我呢？我愛你，也只要你愛我便足矣」。

儘管如此，賽姬還是好奇她的丈夫長什麼樣子。因此，有一天晚上，等到丘比特入睡後，賽姬點亮燈火，看到丘比特俊俏的臉龐。但是一滴滾燙的燈油卻不小心落在丘比特身上，驚醒了丘比特。

丘比特悲傷地說：「我要的只是你的信任。沒有了信任，愛也將消逝。」於是丘比特就飛走了。

• Main Idea and Details

1 (c)　2 (a)　3 (b)　4 (b)　5 (c)
6 a. ugliest　b. Psyche　c. face　d. Cupid

• Vocabulary Builder

1 curious 好奇的　　2 take aim 瞄準
3 prick 刺；扎　　4 depart 離開

Vocabulary Review 8

A
1 Mount Olympus　2 normal
3 heavens　4 monsters
5 punished　6 demigods
7 snakes　8 bull

B
1 spread　2 worshipped
3 Roman　4 Venus
5 Psyche　6 Cupid
7 fell in love　8 curious

C
1 immortal 不死的；長生的　2 messenger 信差；使者
3 Venus 維納斯，美和愛之女神　4 slip 滑落；鬆脫
5 Medusa 瑪杜莎　6 Minotaur 米諾陶洛斯

D
1 正常的 b　2 不死的；長生的 e
3 泰坦 g　4 半人半神 i
5 信奉；敬神 c　6 莫丘利，神的信使 j
7 普路托，冥界之神 f　8 瞄準 a
9 刺；扎 d　10 叫醒 h

33 Architecture and Architects 建築學和建築師

建築學是一種建築設計的藝術，設計建築物的人稱為建築師。

建築師試著設計出兼具美觀與實用的建築。典型來說，他們會確定建築物是對稱的。如果某個物體是對稱的，兩個半部的大小和形狀會完全相同。對稱能使建築物美觀。最有名的對稱建築物之一，就是古希臘的帕德嫩神殿。

有些建築師會添加圓柱、圓頂和拱門，使建築更加優美。古希臘人設計出許多美麗的神殿，當中尤其運用了圓柱的設計。而圓頂是圓形的屋頂，拱門是頂部呈圓弧狀的建築結構。

建築師會在設計上使用各種材料，他們可能會使用木頭或磚塊，也可能使用水泥、混凝土、石頭、鋼鐵甚至是玻璃。多虧了建築師，我們才有這些形形色色的建築物。

• Main Idea and Details

1 (c)　2 (c)　3 (a)　4 (b)
5 a. An architect designs buildings.
b. It has two halves that are exactly the same size and shape.
c. They might be wood, bricks, cement, concrete, stone, steel, and glass.
6 a. architects　b. halves　c. bricks　d. glass

• Vocabulary Builder

1 column 圓柱；柱子　　2 architect 建築師
3 symmetrical/symmetric 對稱的　　4 brick 磚塊

34 Sculptures and Sculptors 雕刻和雕刻家

許多藝術家喜歡繪畫，但是有些則偏好運用材料創作物品勝於繪畫。創作雕刻的藝術家稱為雕刻家。

雕刻是雕刻家所創作的雕像，它們可以非常的小，也可能相當大。雕刻家創作許多不同的雕刻作品，有時候是馬匹等動物雕像，有時可能是男女雕像。《米洛的維納斯》是著名的維納斯古雕像，米開朗基羅的《大衛像》則是世界上最著名的雕刻作品之一。

藝術家使用各式各樣的材料來雕刻，通常石頭是他們偏愛的材料。最常被使用的石材是大理石，它是一種白色堅硬的石頭，可創造出美麗的雕刻作品。也有藝術家使用黏土來雕刻，有些甚至會用金屬或其他材料。

• Main Idea and Details

1 **(a)** 2 **(b)** 3 **(a)** 4 **(a)**

5 a. **Sculptors** b. **statues** c. **materials**

6 a. **tiny** b. **animals** c. **marble** d. **clay**

• Vocabulary Builder

1 **sculpture** 雕刻品；雕像 2 **sculptor** 雕刻家

3 **metal** 金屬 4 **marble** 大理石

35 Elements of Music 音樂的元素

音樂家經常一起演奏，他們可能組成管弦樂隊或交響樂隊。當音樂家一起演奏時，必須同時演奏出正確的樂曲，否則會不好聽。因此會由一名指揮家帶領演奏者，幫助他們合拍並且和諧演奏出樂曲。

音樂家必須能夠看懂樂譜，一首樂曲裡的每個音是由音符來表示，一個音符裡面包含了這個音的音高和音長。

音符寫在五線譜上，有全音符、二分音符、四分音符和八分音符。這些音符標示出每個音必須持續的長度，也標示出音樂家們必須演奏出的聲音類型。

另外還有全休止符、二分休止符、四分休止符和八分休止符。休止符告訴音樂家在這個拍子上要靜音和暫停。全休止符的長度和全音符相同，其他的休止符也是一樣。

• Main Idea and Details

1 **(a)** 2 **(a)** 3 **(c)** 4 **(b)** 5 **(c)**

6 a. **orchestra** b. **conductor** c. **whole**
d. **length** e. **rest**

• Vocabulary Builder

1 **harmony** 和諧；協調 2 **staff** 五線譜

3 **(musical) notes** 音符 4 **pitch** 音高

36 What's Your Vocal Range? 你屬於哪種音域？

男人和女人的聲音不同，音域也不同。

一個人的音域，指的是他或她能唱到多高或多低的音。聲音高亢的人可以唱高音，聲音低沉的人可以唱低音。一般來說，男人的聲音低，女人的聲音高。

我們可以將男聲分為三種類型，男高音是男人所能唱到的最高音，許多著名的歌劇演唱家都是唱男高音。男中音是一般的男聲，大部分男性都屬於男中音。最低的男聲叫做男低音。

至於女聲也可分為三種類型，女高音是女人可以唱到的最高音，許多女歌劇演唱家是女高音。次女高音是一般的女聲，大多數女性唱歌都屬於次女高音。女低音則是女性可以唱到的最低音。

• Main Idea and Details

1 **(a)** 2 **(b)** 3 **(a)** 4 **(c)**

5 a. **notes** b. **baritone** c. **mezzo-soprano**

6 a. **male** b. **average** c. **high** d. **lowest**

• Vocabulary Builder

1 **vocal range** 音域 2 **tenor** 男高音

3 **alto** 女低音 4 **mezzo-soprano** 次女高音；女中音

Vocabulary Review 9

A 1 **designs** 2 **symmetrical**
3 **architecture** 4 **columns**
5 **sculptures** 6 **incredibly**
7 **ancient** 8 **materials**

B 1 **musicians** 2 **in harmony**
3 **represented** 4 **rest sign**
5 **vocal range** 6 **how**
7 **baritone** 8 **female**

C 1 **architecture** 建築學
2 **symmetrical/symmetric** 對稱的
3 **arch** 拱形 4 **statue** 雕像
5 **keep time** 合拍 6 **bass** 男低音

D 1 建築師 **f** 2 雕刻品；雕像 **i**
3 雕刻家 **g** 4 非常；極為 **d**
5 合拍 **b** 6 五線譜 **h**
7 音域 **j** 8 女子；女性 **a**
9 男低音 **c** 10 次女高音；女中音 **e**

Wrap-Up Test 3

A 1 **endpoints** 2 **vertical line**
3 **parallel lines** 4 **based on**
5 **Mount Olympus** 6 **Titans**
7 **worshipped** 8 **fell in love**
9 **sculptors** 10 **vocal range**

B 1 多邊形 2 直角
3 銳角 4 垂直線

5 相交；交叉

6 線段

7 公制單位系統

8 容量

9 應用題

10 計畫

11 正常的

12 不死的；長生的

13 泰坦

14 半人半神

15 信奉；敬神

16 莫丘利，神的信使

17 普路托，冥界之神

18 瞄準

19 刺；扎

20 叫醒

21 魔力；法力

22 建築學

23 對稱的

24 雕像

25 音符

26 休止符

27 雕刻品；雕像

28 非常；極為

29 合拍

30 五線譜

FUN學美國英語閱讀課本 4
各學科實用課文

Authors

Michael A. Putlack
Michael A. Putlack graduated from Tufts University in Medford, Massachusetts, USA, where he got his B.A. in History and English and his M.A. in History. He has written a number of books for children, teenagers, and adults.

e-Creative Contents
A creative group that develops English contents and products for ESL and EFL students.

作者	Michael A. Putlack & e-Creative Contents
翻譯	丁宥暄
編輯	丁宥榆／丁宥暄
校對	陳慧莉
製程管理	洪巧玲
發行人	黃朝萍
出版者	寂天文化事業股份有限公司
電話	+886-(0)2-2365-9739
傳真	+886-(0)2-2365-9835
網址	www.icosmos.com.tw
讀者服務	onlineservice@icosmos.com.tw
出版日期	2023 年 6 月 二版再刷 （寂天雲隨身聽 APP 版）

國家圖書館出版品預行編目 (CIP) 資料

FUN 學美國英語閱讀課本 4 : 各學科實用課文 (寂天雲隨身聽 APP 版) / Michael A. Putlack, e-Creative Contents 著 ; 丁宥暄 , 鄭玉瑋譯 . -- 二版 . -- [臺北市] : 寂天文化 , 2021.09- 冊； 公分

ISBN 978-626-300-049-0 (第 4 冊 : 菊 8K 平裝)

1. 英語 2. 讀本

805.18 110012751

郵撥帳號 1998620-0 寂天文化事業股份有限公司
訂書金額未滿 1000 元，請外加運費 100 元。
〔若有破損，請寄回更換，謝謝。〕

FUN學 美國英語閱讀課本 4

各學科實用課文 二版

Workbook

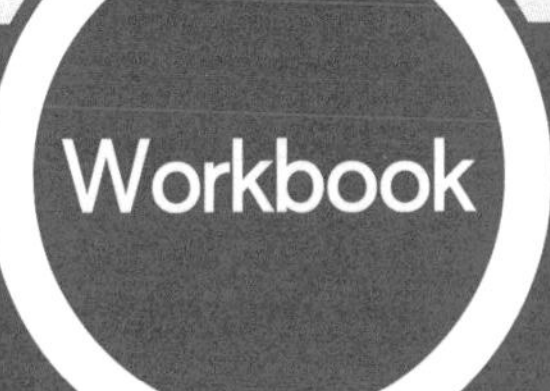

AMERICAN SCHOOL TEXTBOOK

READING KEY

作者 Michael A. Putlack & e-Creative Contents　譯者 丁宥暄

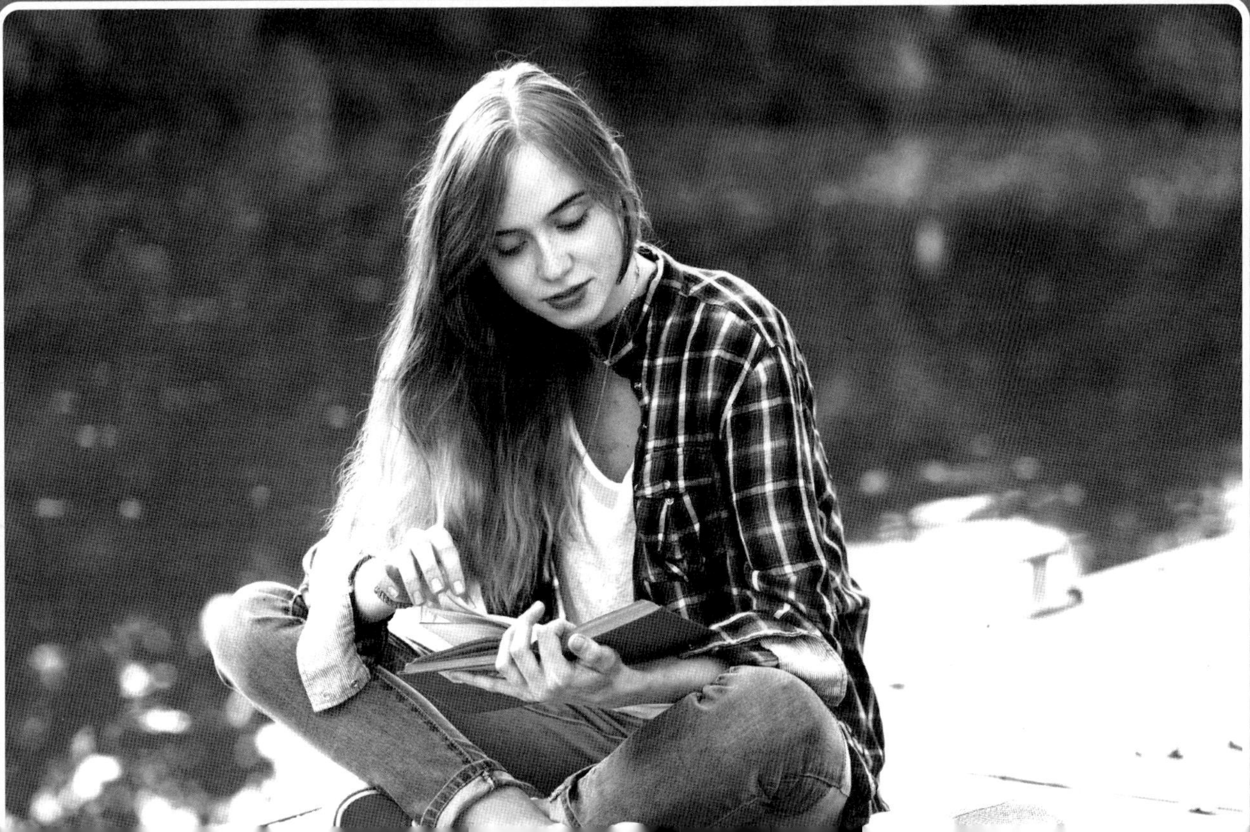

Daily Test 01 Moving to a New Community

A **Listen to the passage and fill in the blanks.** 37

Some people live in the same places for their __________ lives. They grow up, find jobs, and become old in ________ __________ city or town.

But other people move from __________ to place. They move to a ___________ city or another state. Some people even move to different countries. We call these people ______________.

So why do people move to a new _______________? Mostly, they are looking for _________________ to improve their lives. An opportunity is a chance for something __________ to happen. People often move to find a better life for _______________ or their children. And some people even move to another country to seek ____________.

So what can people do in a new community? They can find new _______, get a better education, or make friends. They can also try to _________ a part of it. They should _________ the community's laws and respect other people so that the community becomes a good place ______ _______.

B **Write the meaning of each word or phrase from Word List (main book p.104) in English.**

1 全部的；整個的	__________	8 改進；改善	__________
2 生命；人生	__________	9 尋找；追求	__________
3 成長	__________	10 自由	__________
4 附近的	__________	11 教育	__________
5 移民	__________	12 交朋友	__________
6 尋找	__________	13 服從；遵守	__________
7 機會	__________	14 以便	__________

▶解答請參照主冊課文及 Word List

Daily Test

02 A Nation of Immigrants

A Listen to the passage and fill in the blanks. 38

The United States is a __________ of immigrants. People __________ to the U.S. from all over the world.

In the early __________, many immigrants came from Europe. They __________ on ships across the Atlantic Ocean. They often arrived at __________ __________ in New York Harbor. In New York Harbor, the __________ __________ Liberty greeted them. For many immigrants, "Lady Liberty" was __________ __________ thing they saw in America. It was a __________ of freedom to these immigrants.

In the __________, many immigrants came from Asia. They often arrived at __________ Island in San Francisco Bay.

Moving to another country is not always easy. Immigrants have to __________ __________ to their new __________. They often have to start a __________ new way of life. They have to learn about a new culture and find new jobs and __________. They need to learn a new language __________ __________.

Some immigrants live with the same __________ group. Ethnic __________ can help them get used to their new country.

B Write the meaning of each word or phrase from Word List in English.

1 移民國家 __________

2 遷移；遷入 __________

3 1900 年代 __________

4 航行 __________

5 大西洋 __________

6 自由女神像 __________

7 問候；迎接 __________

8 象徵 __________

9 1960 年代 __________

10 習慣於 __________

11 完整地；完全地 __________

12 族群 __________

Daily Test 03 Earning, Spending, and Saving Money

A Listen to the passage and fill in the blanks.

39

We use money to buy __________ and services. When people work, they get paid. This money gives them an __________. The money that people earn from working is called their __________.

People often do two __________ with their income: They spend it or __________ it. People spend their money on __________ things. These include housing, food, ________________, clothes, and entertainment.

Most people try to spend ________ money than they earn. To do this, they often make a __________. A budget is a plan that shows income, spending, and __________. It is important to make a budget to __________ spending. With a budget, people can plan to buy something and __________ their income and spending.

Many people save money to use ________. If they do not save it, they ________ ________ have any money when they need it. People often __________ that money in a bank.

B Write the meaning of each word or phrase from Word List in English.

1	商品；貨物	______________	9	運輸工具	______________
2	服務	______________	10	娛樂；消遣	______________
3	領薪水；獲得薪資	______________	11	預算	______________
4	收入；所得	______________	12	編列預算	______________
5	賺得	______________	13	開銷；花費	______________
6	收入；薪資	______________	14	存款；積蓄	______________
7	儲蓄	______________	15	使平衡	______________
8	房屋、住房總稱	______________	16	存款（於銀行）	______________

Daily Test 04 Our Needs and Wants

A Listen to the passage and fill in the blanks.

40

People sometimes ____________ more money than they earn. When this happens, they go into __________. Most people try to ___________ going into debt. So they spend their money ______________.

They divide the things they spend money on into two _______________: needs and wants. Needs are things that people __________ ________ to live. Wants are things that people ___________ to have but do not need in order to live.

Needs are more important than ___________. So people spend money on them _________. What are some needs? Housing, food, and ____________ are three important needs. Everyone needs a home to live in, food to eat, and clothes to __________.

What are some ___________? Entertainment and ______________ are wants. So are eating out and _______________.

People cannot buy ________________ that they want. They often have to make _____________. They need to think about _________________ cost. In other words, if they spend money on one thing, they may not buy _____________. Opportunity cost can help people make wise _______________ choices.

B Write the meaning of each word or phrase from Word List in English.

1 債務；借款 ________________

2 負債 ________________

3 避免 ________________

4 小心謹慎地；仔細地 ________________

5 種類；類型 ________________

6 需求 ________________

7 欲求 ________________

8 渴望 ________________

9 為了 ________________

10 娛樂；消遣 ________________

11 外出用餐 ________________

12 社交 ________________

13 機會成本 ________________

14 經濟上的 ________________

Daily Test

05 World Climate Regions

A Listen to the passage and fill in the blanks.

41

Our planet is very large and ___________. So it has many different ___________. Climate refers to the weather ___________ in an area. There are three ___________ climates. They are tropical, ___________, and polar climates.

Tropical climates have hot ___________ all year round. Tropical climates are found near the ___________. Many times, these areas get ________ ___ rain. There are often rain forests in places with ___________ climates.

Polar climates have cold weather ________ ________ round. Polar climates are found in places like ___________ and parts of Russia and Canada. They ________ a lot of snow and ice.

Most of the ___________ has a temperate climate. It does not ______ too hot or too cold in temperate climates. These regions experience four ___________ seasons. Temperate climates have many different _______. Sometimes, they have dry woodlands and ___________. Sometimes, they have ___________ forests that lose their leaves in the fall. They also have ___________ forests. These are forests of evergreens that keep their ___________ during the winter.

B Write the meaning of each word or phrase from Word List in English.

1 行星 ___________

2 多樣的 ___________

3 氣候 ___________

4 指的是 ___________

5 主要的；重要的 ___________

6 熱帶氣候 ___________

7 溫帶氣候 ___________

8 寒帶氣候 ___________

9 全年；一年到頭 ___________

10 赤道 ___________

11 南極洲 ___________

12 經歷；體驗 ___________

13 有區別的；明顯的 ___________

14 林地 ___________

15 大草原 ___________

16 闊葉林 ___________

17 針葉林 ___________

18 常綠樹 ___________

Daily Test

06 Extreme Weather Conditions

A Listen to the passage and fill in the blanks.

42

We usually ______________ normal weather conditions. But, sometimes the weather may become ___________. In these cases, people experience ____________ forms of weather.

Extreme weather can be ______________. There are many ________ ______ extreme weather.

In winter, sometimes the snow ________ so hard that it is impossible to see anything ___________ _______ the color white. This is a blizzard. ____________ can drop huge amounts of snow at one time.

Tropical storms have high winds, heavy rain, ____________, and lightning. Hurricanes and _____________ are two types of these storms. __________ are another kind of storm. These are twisters that have winds that blow _____________ quickly. They can cause a lot of ____________.

Floods and droughts are other examples of natural ___________. Tropical storms and heavy monsoon rains often cause __________. ____________ areas get no rain for a long time. The plants there die, and the soil __________ __________.

B Write the meaning of each word or phrase from Word List in English.

1 正常的；標準的 ________________

2 強烈的；劇烈的 ________________

3 極端的；激烈的 ________________

4 除了……之外 ________________

5 暴風雪 ________________

6 熱帶風暴 ________________

7 雷；雷聲 ________________

8 閃電 ________________

9 颶風 ________________

10 颱風 ________________

11 龍捲風 ________________

12 旋風；龍捲風 ________________

13 極端地；激烈地 ________________

14 破壞 ________________

15 乾旱 ________________

16 自然災害；天然災害 ________________

17 雨季 ________________

18 吹散；隨風而去 ________________

Daily Test

07 Goods and Resources

A **Listen to the passage and fill in the blanks.** 43

There are many kinds of natural __________ on the earth. People use natural resources to __________ goods.

Trees are used to ________ our homes and buildings. Oil that is __________ from the ground is made into fuel and other ________ we use every day. Minerals, such as gold and salt, are also very important _________ resources.

We can divide the _________ resources into ___________ and nonrenewable resources.

Renewable resources can be used again and again. Water, soil, and ________ are renewable resources. Also, ________ _________ and wind power are renewable resources. They can be ________ within a short time.

Nonrenewable resources are the __________. We can only use them once, and then they are gone _________. Many energy resources, such as oil, coal, and natural gas, are ______________ resources. They are _________ in supply and cannot be replaced easily.

We must conserve our natural resources so that we do not _____ _______ _____ them.

B **Write the meaning of each word or phrase from Word List in English.**

1 自然資源 ______________	8 取代；恢復 ______________
2 用幫浦抽出 ______________	9 相反的 ______________
3 礦物 ______________	10 限制 ______________
4 可再生的；可更新的 ______________	11 對於……是有限的 ______________
5 不可再生的；不可更新的 ______________	12 供給；供應 ______________
6 太陽能 ______________	13 保存；保護 ______________
7 風力 ______________	14 將……用完 ______________

Daily Test

08 Goods and Services

A **Listen to the passage and fill in the blanks.** 44

Companies and ____________ make goods such as cars, computers, and furniture. Farmers grow __________ in soil. Then, they sell these __________ to customers.

Goods are things made or __________ for sale. ______________, books, and ice cream are all goods. Any person or company that makes goods is a ____________. Producers try to ________ their goods to people. We call the people who ____________ goods consumers.

Some people ___________ services for others. Waiters, cooks, travel agents, and bus and taxi drivers all have service jobs. Together, goods and services are called ____________.

Most ______________ make goods and provide services to make a profit. Profit is the income a business has left after all its _________ are paid. So, how do businesses make a _________? They can earn a profit if they sell their products at higher __________ than it costs to provide them.

B **Write the meaning of each word or phrase from Word List in English.**

1	工廠	____________	7	消費者	____________
2	農作物；莊稼	____________	8	旅行社職員	____________
3	顧客	____________	9	產品；產物	____________
4	賣；出售	____________	10	利潤；收益	____________
5	生產者；製造者	____________	11	費用；成本；花費	____________
6	買；購買	____________	12	被支付	____________

Daily Test 09 American State and Local Governments

A **Listen to the passage and fill in the blanks.** 45

The United States has __________ types of government. They include local, state, and national __________.

Local governments __________ in towns, cities, and counties. State governments are __________ for governing their states. And the national, or __________, government is responsible for the entire country.

Local governments provide services for the people in their __________. Mostly, they take care of schools, fire departments, and police __________.

State governments __________ an entire state. They are based in the state __________. For example, Boston, Massachusetts, and Atlanta, __________, are the capitals of their states. The state government is responsible for __________ the state's laws.

The national government is __________ in Washington, D.C. Most importantly, the national government is responsible for __________ all Americans safe. It is in charge of national __________. But the government __________ other things, too. It makes and enforces the __________ laws. And it builds __________ such as interstates and highways.

B **Write the meaning of each word or phrase from Word List in English.**

1	幾個的；數個的	__________	9	統治；管理	__________
2	地方政府	__________	10	根基於…… 之內	__________
3	州政府	__________	11	州府	__________
4	聯邦政府	__________	12	實施；執行	__________
5	對…… 有責任的	__________	13	負責	__________
6	照顧	__________	14	安全；防護	__________
7	消防局	__________	15	公共建設	__________
8	警察局	__________	16	州際公路	__________

Daily Test

10 The Three Branches of Government

A Listen to the passage and fill in the blanks. 46

The Constitution is the ____________ law of the USA. It divides the government into three ____________ branches. They are the executive, legislative, and judicial ____________. Each branch has different duties and ____________.

The head of the ____________ branch is the president. The president ____________ the country's laws. The president cannot do this ________. So many people __________ for him. The FBI, CIA, and Department of ____________ are all part of the executive branch. Together, they __________ ________ the nation's laws.

The legislative branch is Congress. ____________ is divided into two houses. The upper house is the ___________, and the lower house is the House of Representatives. Congress's _________ is to make the country's laws.

The ___________ branch is the court system. The ____________ Court is the nation's highest court. But there are many lower courts all ______________ the country. These courts ______________ if people have broken the law or not.

B Write the meaning of each word or phrase from Word List in English.

1 美國憲法 ____________________

2 分；分割 ____________________

3 獨立的；單獨的 ____________________

4 分部；部門 ____________________

5 行政部門 ____________________

6 立法部門 ____________________

7 司法部門 ____________________

8 本分；義務 ____________________

9 責任 ____________________

10 國防部 ____________________

11 進行；實行；執行 ____________________

12 議會；國會 ____________________

13 （美）參議院 ____________________

14 （美）眾議院 ____________________

15 任務；作用；職責 ____________________

16 法院制度 ____________________

17 最高法院 ____________________

18 違反法律 ____________________

Daily Test 11

Laws and Rules

A Listen to the passage and fill in the blanks. 47

Every citizen has many __________ and responsibilities.

The Constitution ____________ the rights that all Americans have. For example, Americans have the right to freedom of speech, _________, and the press. They also have many _________ rights.

However, Americans also have many __________________. For instance, they have to _________ all of the laws in the country. There are many ___________ laws. There are also _________ laws and local laws.

Unfortunately, people sometimes __________ the law. When people break the law, they must often go to __________. If they are found __________, they may get punished.

There are several different kinds of _______________. For small problems, people might have to ________ _____ ________ or do community service. For more serious ___________, they may have to spend time in jail. And, in __________ cases, such as murder, some people may get a lifetime prison sentence or the ________ _________.

B Write the meaning of each word or phrase from Word List in English.

1 權利	______	10 繳交罰款	______
2 言論自由	______	11 社區服務	______
3 宗教自由	______	12 罪；罪行	______
4 新聞自由	______	13 入獄	______
5 不幸地	______	14 嚴重的	______
6 法庭；法院	______	15 謀殺；謀殺案	______
7 有罪的	______	16 案件；訴訟	______
8 受到懲罰	______	17 終生監禁；無期徒刑	______
9 處罰；懲罰	______	18 死刑	______

Daily Test

12 The Jury System

A Listen to the passage and fill in the blanks.

48

The Constitution ________ all Americans the right to a trial by jury. In the United States, ________ ________ are an important part of the justice system.

A jury is made up of ________ citizens. It can be ________ ____ anyone, such as businessmen, housewives, doctors, or college students.

There are two kinds of juries: a grand jury and a ________ ________.

Grand juries usually have _____ to _____ members. They decide if there is enough ________ to have a trial. If there is enough evidence, they ________ _____ have a trial. If there is not enough evidence, they vote ________ having a trial. Then, there will be no ________.

Petit juries decide actual ________ cases. They usually have 12 ________. The petit jury listens to the ________ and defendant during the trial. Each trial has a ________, too. The judge helps the case proceed ________. At the end of the trial, the jury decides on a ________. It decides if the ________ is guilty or not guilty.

B Write the meaning of each word or phrase from Word List in English.

1 審問；審判 ________

2 陪審團 ________

3 普通的；一般的 ________

4 由……所組成 ________

5 由……所構成 ________

6 大陪審團 ________

7 小陪審團 ________

8 證據 ________

9 投票表決 ________

10 投票反對 ________

11 刑事案件 ________

12 檢察官 ________

13 被告 ________

14 法官 ________

15 繼續進行 ________

16 平穩地；順利地 ________

17 在……的末尾 ________

18 （陪審團的）裁定；裁決 ________

Daily Test

13 Kinds of Plants

A Listen to the passage and fill in the blanks.

49

There are many __________ of plants. However, scientists divide them into two main __________. These are _____________ plants and conifers.

The main difference _____________ them is how they produce their seeds. A plant's seeds are what let it ______________.

Flowering plants have flowers and produce __________ in flowers. Most plants are flowering __________. They include peas, strawberries, cherries, and __________.

Conifers do not have flowers. Instead, they produce their seeds in _________. Pine trees, fir trees, and __________ trees are conifers.

Many conifers are ______________ trees. Evergreen trees have ____________ instead of leaves and stay green all year long.

While most conifers have needles for ___________, the majority of trees are ______________ trees. Deciduous trees have __________ ________ that usually change color in the fall. Also, they drop their leaves in ___________. In spring, the leaves __________ __________ again.

B Write the meaning of each word or phrase from Word List in English.

1	種類	________________	8	冷杉	________________
2	開花植物	________________	9	雲杉	________________
3	針葉植物；針葉樹	________________	10	常綠樹	________________
4	繁殖；生殖	________________	11	針葉	________________
5	碗豆	________________	12	代替	________________
6	毬果；松果	________________	13	落葉樹	________________
7	松樹	________________	14	長出來	________________

Daily Test

14 How Do Plants Make Food?

A Listen to the passage and fill in the blanks.

50

All living things need ____________ to live. Animals eat ____________ to get energy. But plants make their ____________ food. They do this in a ____________ called photosynthesis.

Plants use sunlight ______ ____________ ______ make their food. Leaves are the main ________________ part of a plant.

A leaf is green because it has a ______________ called chlorophyll. _______________ is found in chloroplasts, which are where a plant makes _______ food.

First, when the sun ___________ on a leaf, the chlorophyll absorbs sunlight. Then, the ________________ use carbon dioxide, water, and the sun's energy to make sugar. The __________ is food for the plant. This process is __________________.

As photosynthesis occurs, the plant __________ ______ carbon dioxide from the air. At the same time, the plant __________ ________ oxygen into the air. This is what people ____________. All animals must breathe in ____________ to stay alive. So, ___________ _______ plants, people and animals can live, too.

B Write the meaning of each word or phrase from Word List in English.

1 過程 ____________________

2 光合作用 ____________________

3 為了 ____________________

4 物質 ____________________

5 葉綠素 ____________________

6 葉綠體 ____________________

7 二氧化碳 ____________________

8 糖 ____________________

9 發生 ____________________

10 接受；吸收 ____________________

11 發出；散出 ____________________

12 呼吸；呼氣；吸氣 ____________________

Daily Test 15 Classifications of Animals

A **Listen to the passage and fill in the blanks.** 51

Animals can be grouped according to their ___________. One way to classify animals is by ______________ or not they have backbones.

An animal with a _______________ is called a vertebrate. All mammals, birds, reptiles, fish, and amphibians are _________________.

An animal without a backbone is called an __________________. Invertebrates include insects, flatworms, sponges, shrimp, and ________.

All vertebrates can be ____________ divided into two classes: warm-blooded animals and ___________________ animals.

Warm-blooded animals can ______________ their body temperatures. So, even if it is very cold or very hot outside, their bodies stay the same __________________. Mammals and birds are ___________________________.

Cold-blooded animals need the sun to ___________ their bodies. So their body temperatures can change with the _______________ temperature. These animals often rest in the sun for hours to _________ _______ heat. Reptiles, fish, and _________________ are cold-blooded.

B **Write the meaning of each word or phrase from Word List in English.**

1 根據；按照 ______________________
2 特徵；特點 ______________________
3 將⋯⋯分類 ______________________
4 脊骨；脊柱 ______________________
5 脊椎動物 ______________________
6 爬蟲類動物 ______________________
7 無脊椎動物 ______________________
8 扁蟲 ______________________
9 （海中動物）海綿 ______________________
10 進一步地 ______________________
11 （動物）溫血的；恆溫的 ______________________
12 （動物）冷血的 ______________________
13 調節；控制 ______________________
14 環境 ______________________
15 吸收 ______________________
16 兩棲動物 ______________________

Daily Test

16 What Do Animals Need to Live and Grow?

A Listen to the passage and fill in the blanks. 52

All animals have ________ needs to live and grow. They all need food, water, air, and ________.

All animals need food and water to ________ ________. Food and ________ give an animal energy. Like fuel ________ a machine, all animals need energy to work. As an animal ________, it needs more food and water.

All animals need oxygen to ________. How do animals get ________? Animals that live on land take in oxygen ________ their lungs. But fish and some water animals do not have ________. ________, they breathe with gills to take in oxygen from water.

All animals need a shelter—a place ________ ________. This shelter ________ them safe from the weather and from other animals.

Animals also ________ to changes in their environment to survive. When the weather gets colder, some animals ________ to warmer places. Some animals find places to ________. Cold-blooded animals lie in the sunlight to warm their ________.

B Write the meaning of each word or phrase from Word List in English.

1	基本的；基礎的	________	7	作為替代	________
2	棲身處；避難所	________	8	鰓	________
3	活著；生存	________	9	對…… 作出反應	________
4	運轉	________	10	遷移；遷徙	________
5	經由；透過	________	11	冬眠	________
6	肺	________	12	躺；臥	________

Daily Test 17 What Makes up a Food Chain?

A Listen to the passage and fill in the blanks. 53

Animals __________ make their own food. They get their food by eating other __________. Some animals eat __________. Others eat animals. And most animals are __________ __________ one another on the food chain.

The food chain shows how all organisms are __________ __________ one another for food.

For instance, at the __________ of the food chain, a plant uses the sun to make its own food. Then, a __________ may eat the plant. Next, a __________ may eat the rabbit. Later, a __________ may eat the fox. Finally, the wolf dies, and its body __________. This provides __________ for the ground so that more plants may grow.

All organisms on the planet are producers, consumers, or __________. Producers, like plants, make __________ __________ food. Consumers are organisms that eat producers or other __________. Animals are consumers. And decomposers are organisms that __________ __________, or decompose, other organisms. Together, they all __________ __________ the food chain.

B Write the meaning of each word or phrase from Word List in English.

1 生物；有機體 __________

2 與……連結 __________

3 食物鏈 __________

4 依賴…… __________

5 例如 __________

6 在……底部 __________

7 分解 __________

8 營養物 __________

9 生產者 __________

10 消費者 __________

11 分解者 __________

12 分解 __________

Daily Test 18 Herbivores, Carnivores, and Omnivores

A Listen to the passage and fill in the blanks. 54

All animals need to eat to ______________. Different consumers eat ______________ kinds of food. There are three ____________ of animals according to the food they eat. They are _________________, carnivores, and _________________.

Herbivores are animals that only eat plants. We call these animals plant ____________. There are many ____________ ________ herbivores. They can be small, like rabbits, or they can be big, like ____________. Elephants are herbivores ________ __________. These animals are also often called __________ animals.

Carnivores are ___________ eaters. They often ___________ prey animals and kill other animals. Lions, tigers, and ____________ are dangerous carnivores. Carnivores are often called ________________.

Some animals eat both meat and _________________. We call ________ animals omnivores. _____________ and pigs are omnivores. ___________ are omnivores as well.

Food chains can ______________. They do not follow a single ___________. Several food chains that overlap form a ___________ __________. A food web shows how food chains are _________________.

B Write the meaning of each word or phrase from Word List in English.

1 草食性動物 ______________________

2 肉食性動物 ______________________

3 雜食性動物 ______________________

4 也 ______________________

5 獵物型動物 ______________________

6 掠食者；食肉動物 ______________________

7 重疊 ______________________

8 小路；小徑 ______________________

9 食物網 ______________________

10 連接；結合 ______________________

Daily Test 19 What Are Ecosystems?

A **Listen to the passage and fill in the blanks.** 55

We live in an ________________. An environment is all the living and nonliving things that ______________ us.

Plants and animals ____________ _______ one another in an environment. They depend on nonliving things, too, ________ water, air, and soil. Together, all the living and ______________ things in an area form an ecosystem.

The earth has many different ________________. There are desert, forest, ______________, lake, and ocean ecosystems.

Different kinds of ecosystems are ___________ ________ _______ different kinds of plants and animals. Many trees and animals can be ________ in a forest. A lake is __________ _________ fish, frogs, and insects.

The organisms in these ecosystems ______________ against each other to survive. ___________ plants compete for water. ___________ compete for prey. Prey animals such as rabbits and squirrels compete to ________ food.

Ecosystems are ______________ changing. So the plants and animals must __________ to these changes, too. _______________ that adapt will survive. Organisms that do not adapt ________ ________ survive.

B **Write the meaning of each word or phrase from Word List in English.**

1 環境；自然環境	____________	7 由……組成	____________
2 非生物	____________	8 被找到；被發現	____________
3 圍繞；包圍	____________	9 充滿	____________
4 依賴……	____________	10 競爭；對抗	____________
5 生態系統	____________	11 不斷地；時常地	____________
6 草原	____________	12 適應	____________

Daily Test 20

Dinosaurs: Extinct but Still Popular

A Listen to the passage and fill in the blanks.

56

Ecosystems can ________. When a large change ________, the organisms that live in that ecosystem are ________. Some even have trouble ________.

Do you like ________? They lived on Earth ________ ______ years ago. Some dinosaurs, like brontosaurus and triceratops, were ______. They were herbivores. But there were many vicious ________, too. Velociraptors were ________ predators that hunted in packs. And Tyrannosaurus rex was the most ________ dinosaur of all.

However, around ______ ________ years ago, the dinosaurs suddenly died out. Scientists think that a large ________ hit the earth then. It completely changed the ________. The weather on the earth got colder, and the sun ________ less. The planet's ________ all changed. Many plants and animals ________. The dinosaurs could not adapt, so they became ________, too. No dinosaurs live on ______ now.

Many organisms are ________ extinct even today. If they are not ______ ______ respond to changes in their environment, some ________ animals may perish.

B Write the meaning of each word or phrase from Word List in English.

1 影響 ________
2 有……的困難 ________
3 恐龍 ________
4 草食性動物 ________
5 兇惡的 ________
6 掠食者；食肉動物 ________
7 兇猛的 ________
8 成群 ________
9 可怕的 ________
10 六千五百萬年 ________
11 滅絕；漸漸消失 ________
12 小行星 ________
13 完全地；徹底地 ________
14 絕種；滅絕 ________
15 瀕臨絕種的 ________
16 消亡；毀滅 ________

Daily Test **21**

The Weather

A Listen to the passage and fill in the blanks.

57

The weather is the condition of the ______________. The weather has three main ______________: the temperature, the air pressure, and the wind.

The ______________ tells us how hot or how cold it is. We measure the temperature in ____________. There are two ______________ systems. They are Fahrenheit and ____________. 32° Fahrenheit is the same as ________ Celsius.

The ________ ____________ is the amount of force that is in the air. When there is ________ air pressure, it may rain or snow. When there is high air pressure, the weather is __________ nice.

Wind occurs when the air __________. Sometimes, the wind can _________ very hard. Other times, it __________ ________ blow at all.

The weather is constantly ____________. Meteorologists use many ______________ to measure the weather. Three important ones are ______________, barometers, and anemometers. A thermometer ____________ the air temperature. A ______________ measures the air pressure. And an ______________ measures the speed of the wind.

B Write the meaning of each word or phrase from Word List in English.

1 大氣	______________	8 壓力	______________
2 特徵；特性	______________	9 氣象學者	______________
3 溫度	______________	10 儀器；器具	______________
4 氣壓	______________	11 溫度計	______________
5 度	______________	12 氣壓計	______________
6 華氏溫標	______________	13 風速計	______________
7 攝氏溫標	______________	14 風速	______________

Daily Test 22 The Water Cycle

A **Listen to the passage and fill in the blanks.** 58

There is a __________ amount of water on the earth. However, this water often changes __________. We call these changes the __________ __________.

There are three __________ in the water cycle: evaporation, __________, and precipitation.

There is water in rivers, lakes, and __________. The water is __________. The sun often __________ on this water. The sun's heat causes some of the water to __________. So it turns into water vapor, a __________ form of water.

This __________ __________ rises into the atmosphere. As it gets higher in the air, the temperature __________. So the water vapor __________ and becomes liquid again. These water __________ form into clouds. Actually, clouds are made of __________ __________ water droplets. Sometimes, the clouds become too heavy, so they __________ their water. It falls to the __________ as rain, snow, or ice.

Some water gets __________ into the ground. But, other times, it __________ __________ bodies of water. Then, the water cycle __________ all over again.

B **Write the meaning of each word or phrase from Word List in English.**

1	固定的；不變的	__________	9	水蒸氣	__________
2	型態；形式	__________	10	氣體的；氣態的	__________
3	水循環	__________	11	凝結	__________
4	階段；時期	__________	12	小水滴	__________
5	蒸發	__________	13	釋放	__________
6	凝結	__________	14	被吸收	__________
7	降水	__________	15	流入	__________
8	蒸發	__________	16	水域	__________

Daily Test

23 Rocks, Minerals, and Soil

A Listen to the passage and fill in the blanks.

59

The earth's __________ is made up of rocks, minerals, and soil. There are three major types of __________. They are igneous, sedimentary, and __________________ rocks.

Igneous rocks are very hard. They form when ____________ __________ cools and ____________. Granite and ____________ are igneous rocks.

Sedimentary rocks are much ___________. They form when __________ ______ sand, mud, and pebbles are pressed together. Limestone and ______________ are sedimentary rocks.

Metamorphic rocks are rocks that have ____________ from one type of rock into another. Marble and quartz are ____________ metamorphic rocks.

Rocks are made of many kinds of ______________. A mineral is a solid ______________ found in nature. Minerals can be ______________ like carbon, iron, or gold. Or they can be ____________ like quartz.

Soil is made of many different ______________. These include small _________ _______ rocks and minerals. Silt, clay, sand, and _________ are all soil. We use ________ to grow plants in.

B Write the meaning of each word or phrase from Word List in English.

1 地殼	______________	11 石灰岩	______________
2 礦物	______________	12 沙岩	______________
3 火成岩	______________	13 大理石	______________
4 沉積岩	______________	14 石英	______________
5 變質岩	______________	15 【化】元素	______________
6 變硬；變堅固	______________	16 碳	______________
7 花崗岩	______________	17 水晶	______________
8 玄武岩	______________	18 小片；小塊	______________
9 鵝卵石	______________	19 粉沙；泥沙	______________
10 受到擠壓	______________	20 腐殖質	______________

Daily Test

24 Fossils and Fossil Fuels

A Listen to the passage and fill in the blanks.

60

Woolly ______________ lived thousands of years ago. But they are not ________ on Earth now. The ____________ are also not alive. Then, how do we know __________ them? We _________ about them from their fossils.

What are __________? Fossils are the ___________ of dead plants or animals that lived long ago. It takes them a very long time to _______. Shells, teeth, and __________ can become fossils. A fossil can even be a ____________ or impression in rock. Most fossils are __________ in sedimentary rocks. Fossils are also found in __________.

We get ________ from fossils, too. Coal, oil, and __________ _____ are fossil fuels. Fossil fuels formed from the remains of plants and animals that ________ long ago.

Scientists study fossils because they can learn much about the ______ past from them. Fossils tell us how life on Earth has ____________. Fossils can also tell Earth's __________. We know a lot about the extinct animals and plants _ __________ ______ fossils.

B Write the meaning of each word or phrase from Word List in English.

1 長毛象 ________________

2 活著的 ________________

3 化石 ________________

4 遺體；遺骨 ________________

5 腳印；足跡 ________________

6 壓印；印記 ________________

7 琥珀 ________________

8 化石燃料 ________________

9 絕種的；滅絕的 ________________

10 幸虧；由於 ________________

Daily Test 25 Points, Lines, and Line Segments

A **Listen to the passage and fill in the blanks.** 61

Make a _______ on a piece of paper. _________, make another dot. Now, _________ the two dots. You have just _________ a line. And the two dots are called _________. You can give the points _______ like this:

A B We call _________ point A and point B.

The line that goes __________ points A and B is called line AB. It is _________ like this, too: $\overleftrightarrow{AB}$.

A _________ is a part of something. A _____ segment is a part of a line.

C D A line can go on _________, but a line segment has two endpoints. We call the line segment by its __________ like this: line segment CD or $\overline{CD}$.

Lines can go in many different __________. A horizontal line ______ from left to right. A _________ line goes up and down. A ________ line moves at an angle.

Sometimes, two lines ________ each other. We can say that these lines __________ one another. When a horizontal line and a vertical line intersect, they might form a ________ ________. The two lines that form a right angle are called _____________ lines. If two lines run side by side and never meet, they are _________ lines.

B **Write the meaning of each word or phrase from Word List in English.**

1 點；圓點 __________

2 連接；連結 __________

3 點 __________

4 通過；穿過 __________

5 部分；斷片 __________

6 線段 __________

7 無窮地；繼續地 __________

8 端點 __________

9 水平線 __________

10 垂直線 __________

11 對角線；斜線 __________

12 相交；交叉 __________

13 直角 __________

14 垂直線 __________

15 並排 __________

16 平行線 __________

Daily Test 26 Polygons

A Listen to the passage and fill in the blanks. 62

There are many types of ______________. A polygon is made of three or more _________ ______________. And it must be a ___________ figure. That means all of the lines in the polygon meet ________ ___________.

A polygon with three __________ is a triangle. A polygon with four sides is a ___________ or a rectangle. A ______________ polygon is a pentagon, a six-sided polygon is a _____________, and an eight-sided polygon is an ____________.

When we create a polygon, the lines meet at ___________ points. When two lines meet, they ___________ an angle.

For _____________, there are four sides to a square. So a square has four ___________. Each of these angles is a __________ angle. This means that each angle is _______ degrees. But not _______ polygons have right angles. There are polygons with __________ angles, which are less than 90 ____________. And there are polygons with ___________ angles, ___________ are greater than 90 degrees.

B Write the meaning of each word or phrase from Word List in English.

1 多邊形 ____________________

2 封閉形狀 ____________________

3 邊 ____________________

4 五個邊的 ____________________

5 五邊形 ____________________

6 六邊形 ____________________

7 八邊形 ____________________

8 某幾個；某些 ____________________

9 角度 ____________________

10 直角 ____________________

11 銳角 ____________________

12 小於 ____________________

13 鈍角 ____________________

14 大於 ____________________

Daily Test 27 The U.S. Customary System and the Metric System

A **Listen to the passage and fill in the blanks.** 63

We often need to know the ____________, weight, and capacity of various items. To measure them, we use measurement ____________. There are two major systems: the U.S. ______________ system and the metric system.

The U.S. customary system is __________ in the United States. Most of the world uses the ___________ system. The metric system is _________ _______ units of ten. The U.S. customary system uses different types of ________________.

The metric system uses the ___________ to measure length. For smaller units, there are ______________ and millimeters. For bigger units, there are ____________. The U.S. customary system uses the _______. There are 12 _________ in one foot. For bigger units, it uses the _______.

For ___________, the metric system uses the gram and _____________. The U.S. customary system uses the ounce and the ___________. There are 16 ___________ in one pound.

And for ____________, the metric system uses the liter. The U.S. customary system uses the cup, pint, quart, and ___________.

B **Write the meaning of each word or phrase from Word List in English.**

1 長度 ____________________

2 重量 ____________________

3 容量 ____________________

4 度量系統 ____________________

5 美制單位系統 ____________________

6 公制單位系統 ____________________

7 以……為基礎 ____________________

8 單位 ____________________

9 英尺 ____________________

10 英寸 ____________________

11 品脫 ____________________

12 夸脫 ____________________

Daily Test

28 Measurement Word Problems

A Listen to the passage and fill in the blanks. 64

1. John loves to ________. In the morning, he jogs ________ meters. In the afternoon, he jogs ________ meters. And in the evening, he jogs 800 ________. How many ________ does he jog during the day?

   ⇨ He jogs a ________ of 2,700 meters. There are ________ meters in 1 kilometer. 2,700 ÷ 1,000 = 2.7. So he jogs ________ kilometers.

2. Sally is cutting some ________ for a science project. She needs to have 7 ________ of string. But her ________ only measures inches. How many ________ of string does she need?

   ⇨ There are ________ inches in one foot. 7 × 12 = ________. So she ________ 84 inches of string.

3. James goes to the store to buy some ________. He asks the ________ to give him a pound and a half of ham. How many ________ of ham does he get?

   ⇨ There are ________ ounces in one pound. 1.5 × 16 = 24. He gets ________ ounces of ham.

4. Diana is ________, so she goes to the ________ store for a drink. She buys a ________-milliliter can of soda. How many ________ of soda does she buy?

   ⇨ There are 1,000 ________ in one liter. 500 ÷ 1,000 = 0.5. She buys ________ liters of soda.

B Write the meaning of each word or phrase from Word List in English.

1 應用題	________	5 肉販；屠夫	________
2 慢跑	________	6 便利商店	________
3 線；細繩	________	7 汽水	________
4 計畫	________	8 毫升	________

Daily Test

29 Gods and Goddesses in Greek Myths

A Listen to the passage and fill in the blanks. 65

The ancient __________ believed in many gods and goddesses. They believed the gods and __________ lived on the highest mountain in Greece, called Mount __________. From there, they __________ __________ on the earth and controlled people and nature.

In Greek myths, the gods and goddesses often acted like __________ people. They ate, drank, and __________. They __________ with each other, fell in love, and __________ __________. However, they had magical powers and were __________. They never __________.

Zeus was the most __________ god. He was the king of the gods and ruled the __________. His brother __________ was the god of the sea, and his other brother Hades was the god of the __________.

Hera was Zeus's wife and the goddess of __________. Athena was the goddess of __________, Ares was the god of war, and Aphrodite was the goddess of love and __________. Hermes was the __________ of the gods. Apollo, a son of Zeus, was the god of __________, and his twin sister Artemis was the goddess of the __________.

B Write the meaning of each word or phrase from Word List in English.

1 古代的 __________
2 希臘的；希臘人 __________
3 女神 __________
4 俯瞰 __________
5 正常的 __________
6 爭吵 __________
7 戀愛 __________
8 結婚 __________
9 魔力；法力 __________
10 不死的；長生的 __________
11 天上；眾天神 __________
12 冥界；地獄 __________
13 婚姻 __________
14 信差；使者 __________

Daily Test

30 Titans, Heroes, and Monsters in Greek Myths

A **Listen to the passage and fill in the blanks.** 66

Greek ______________ had many Titans, heroes, and monsters ______ ________ ________ gods.

The __________ were powerful giants that fought, but ________ to, the gods. _________ was the strongest Titan. The gods punished him by making him hold the world up on his _____________. Prometheus was a Titan who ________ fire from the gods and _________ it to the people on Earth.

Greek myths had many ___________, too. These heroes were often _____________. So, one parent was human __________ the other was a god or goddess. The greatest hero of all was ____________. He was a son of Zeus and the _____________ man in the world. Perseus, Theseus, Achilles, and _____________ were heroes, too.

Finally, there were many _____________. Medusa had a woman's head but ___________ for hair. If anyone looked at ____________, the person would turn to stone. The _____________ was a man with the head of a bull. A centaur was part human and part __________. And satyrs were half man and half _________.

B **Write the meaning of each word or phrase from Word List in English.**

1 神話 ____________________

2 泰坦 ____________________

3 怪物；妖怪 ____________________

4 和；還有 ____________________

5 巨人 ____________________

6 打仗；打架 ____________________

7 輸掉 ____________________

8 托住；支撐 ____________________

9 半人半神 ____________________

10 而；然而 ____________________

11 梅杜莎（女人頭蛇髮妖）____________

12 米諾陶洛斯（人身牛頭怪）__________

13 半人馬（半人半馬怪）_____________

14 薩特（半人半羊怪）_______________

Daily Test 31 Same Gods, Different Names

A **Listen to the passage and fill in the blanks.** 67

The ancient Greeks ___________ their culture to many other places. One of these places was the ___________ Empire. The gods and goddesses of the ancient Greeks were also ___________ by the people of ancient Rome.

The Romans did not use the Greek names ___________. Instead, they gave their gods new ___________.

Zeus was the ___________ of the gods in Greek mythology. But in Roman mythology, his name was ___________. Poseidon was the ___________ god of the sea. But his Roman name was ___________. And Hades was the Greek god of the ___________. But the Romans called him ___________.

The other gods and ___________ got new names, too. Hera, the wife of Zeus, became ___________. Athena, the goddess of wisdom, became ___________. Ares, the god of war, became ___________. Aphrodite, the goddess of love and beauty, became ___________. Artemis, the goddess of the hunt, was ___________. Hermes, the messenger of the gods, was ___________. But, Apollo, the god of light, was ___________ the same name: ___________.

B **Write the meaning of each word or phrase from Word List in English.**

1 傳播；散佈 ___________

2 羅馬帝國 ___________

3 信奉；敬神 ___________

4 然而；還是 ___________

5 朱比特（眾神之王） ___________

6 涅普頓（海神） ___________

7 普路托（冥王） ___________

8 馬爾斯（戰神） ___________

9 維納斯（美和愛之女神） ___________

10 莫丘利（神的信使） ___________

Daily Test

32 Cupid and Psyche

A **Listen to the passage and fill in the blanks.** 68

Once there was a beautiful ____________ named Psyche. Some people said she was more ____________ than Venus, the goddess of love and beauty.

Venus was ____________, so she said to her son Cupid, "Shoot the girl with your ____________ and make her fall in love with the ________ man on Earth."

Cupid took his bow and arrow and ________ ________ to Earth. Just as he was taking aim to shoot Psyche, his finger ____________. He got pricked with his own arrow and fell in love with ____________.

They got married. But Cupid came to Psyche only ________ she slept. He stayed ________ ________, but left before morning's light. One night, Psyche asked Cupid why he came in ____________. "Why should you ________ to see me?" he answered. "I love you, and all I _____ is that you love me."

Still, Psyche was so ____________ who her husband was. So, one night Psyche waited until ____________ fell asleep. She ________ a lamp and saw the lovely face of Cupid. But a drop of hot oil fell from the lamp and ____________ Cupid.

"I asked only for your ________," he said sadly. "When trust is gone, love must ____________." And Cupid ________ ________.

B **Write the meaning of each word or phrase from Word List in English.**

1 妒忌的 ____________

2 射中；射傷 ____________

3 箭 ____________

4 最醜的 ____________

5 弓 ____________

6 飛下來 ____________

7 瞄準 ____________

8 滑落；鬆脫 ____________

9 刺；扎 ____________

10 漆黑 ____________

11 好奇的 ____________

12 睡著 ____________

13 點燃；點燈 ____________

14 滴；一滴 ____________

15 叫醒 ____________

16 信任；信賴 ____________

17 離去 ____________

18 飛走 ____________

Daily Test

33 Architecture and Architects

A Listen to the passage and fill in the blanks.

69

Architecture is the art of ______________ buildings. A person who designs buildings is called an ______________.

Architects try to design buildings that both look nice and are __________. Typically, they try to __________ __________ that their buildings are symmetrical. If something is ________________, it has two halves that are exactly the same size and shape. Symmetry makes buildings ______ nice. One of the most famous examples of symmetric ______________ is the Parthenon from ancient Greece.

Some architects add _____________, domes, and arches to their buildings to make them look better. The ancient Greeks designed many beautiful _____________, especially ones with columns. A dome is a __________________ roof. An arch is a structure that is ____________ at the top.

Architects use all kinds of ______________ in their designs. They might use wood or ___________. They can also use cement, concrete, stone, steel, and even ________. Thanks to architects, we have a wide _________ _____ buildings that all look different from one another.

B Write the meaning of each word or phrase from Word List in English.

1 建築學	________	9 帕特農神殿	________
2 建築師	________	10 圓柱；柱形物	________
3 實用的	________	11 圓蓋；圓屋頂	________
4 典型地；一般地	________	12 拱形；拱門	________
5 對稱的	________	13 神殿；廟宇	________
6 一半；二分之一	________	14 建築；構造	________
7 完全地	________	15 磚塊	________
8 對稱	________	16 各種各樣的	________

Daily Test 34 Sculptures and Sculptors

A Listen to the passage and fill in the blanks. 70

Many ________ paint or draw. But some prefer to make things with materials ________ ________ paint. Artists who make sculptures are called ________.

________ are statues that sculptors make. They can be ________ tiny, or they can be quite large. Sculptors make many different ________ of sculptures. Sometimes, they make ________ of animals, like horses. ________ ________, they might make statues of men and women. The *Venus de Milo* is a famous ________ sculpture of Venus. And *David*, by Michelangelo, is one of the ________ ________ sculptures in the world.

To make sculptures, artists use many different types of ________. They often ________ stone. ________ is the most common stone they use. It is a hard, white ________. And it ________ beautiful sculptures. Other artists use ________ to make sculptures. And some of them even use ________ or other types of materials.

B Write the meaning of each word or phrase from Word List in English.

1 繪畫 ________

2 畫 ________

3 偏好 ________

4 除了 ________

5 雕刻品；雕像 ________

6 雕刻家 ________

7 雕像 ________

8 非常；極為 ________

9 極小的；微小的 ________

10 很；相當 ________

Daily Test

35 Elements of Music

A **Listen to the passage and fill in the blanks.** 71

_______________ often play together. They may do this in an orchestra or a _______________. When the musicians play together, they should play the _____________ music at the same time. If they do not, their music will ____________ bad. So a _______________ leads the musicians. The conductor helps them keep time and play _______ ______________ with one another.

The musicians must be able to __________ music. Each sound in a piece of music is _________________ by a musical note. A musical note includes the __________ and length of the musical sound.

Notes are written on a __________. There are whole notes, half notes, quarter notes, and ____________ notes. These notes indicate the length of time each note must _________. The notes also _____________ the type of sound that the musician must make.

There are also ___________ ___________, half rests, quarter rests, and eighth rests. The rest sign tells the musician to keep quiet and to _________ during that beat. A whole rest lasts the same _____________ _____ time as a whole note. So do the other __________.

B **Write the meaning of each word or phrase from Word List in English.**

1 音樂家；演奏家	____________	9 五線譜	____________
2 指揮家	____________	10 全音符	____________
3 合拍	____________	11 二分音符	____________
4 和諧；協調	____________	12 四分音符	____________
5 讀樂譜	____________	13 八分音符	____________
6 以……表現	____________	14 指出；標出	____________
7 音符	____________	15 持續；延續	____________
8 音高	____________	16 休止符	____________

Daily Test

36 What's Your Vocal Range?

A Listen to the passage and fill in the blanks.

72

Men's voices and women's __________ sound different from one another. Men and women have a different __________ __________.

A __________ vocal range is how high and low he or she can sing. A person with a high voice can sing high __________. A person with a __________ __________ can sing low notes. Usually, men's voices are low while women's voices are __________.

We can divide men's voices into three __________. Tenor is the highest voice that a __________ can sing. Many famous __________ singers sing tenor. Baritone is an __________ male voice. Most males sing in the __________ voice. The lowest male voice is called the __________.

As for __________, there are three categories for their voices, too. Soprano is the highest voice that a __________ can sing. Many female opera singers are __________. __________ is the average female voice. Most females sing in the mezzo-soprano __________. And __________ is the lowest voice that a woman can sing.

B Write the meaning of each word or phrase from Word List in English.

1	聽起來	__________	7	一般的；中等的	__________
2	音域	__________	8	男低音	__________
3	男高音	__________	9	女高音	__________
4	男性；男性的	__________	10	女性；女性的	__________
5	歌劇演唱家	__________	11	次女高音；女中音	__________
6	男中音	__________	12	女低音	__________

MEMO